NO ONE COULD RESIST CHRISTINA'S TOUCH

CARL STANOWSKI
He was a scientist who believed in better loving through chemistry, and Christina's physiology became his speciality.

HELEN STANOWSKI
The doctor whose examinations of Christina were always intensely physical—in and out of the lab.

MARK BERNSTEIN
A rock star who wanted Christina to join his sextet, after they had the chance to make beautiful music together.

ROBERT FRENCH
No case was more trying than this lawyer's attempt to defend himself against Christina's irresistible appeal.

CHRISTINA MAKES LOVE USING ALL FIVE SENSES, BUT NOTHING FEELS BETTER THAN HER TOUCH.

GW00578082

CHRISTINA'S TOUCH

Blakely St James

ARROW BOOKS

Arrow Books Limited
62-65 Chandos Place, London WC2N 4NW

An imprint of Century Hutchinson Limited

London Melbourne Sydney Auckland
Johannesburg and agencies throughout
the world

First published in Great Britain 1987

Printed and bound in Great Britain by
Anchor Brendon Limited, Tiptree, Essex

ISBN 0 09 951700 0

CHAPTER ONE

I woke up feeling sexy all over. My face felt flushed, as though I had a fever, and my nipples were tight and erect. My breasts were so sensitive that just the touch of them against the white silk sheets of my bed sent little tingles and shivers running through my body.

I turned over in bed, moving carefully so as not to wake Gary, who was lying beside me. I felt embarrassed by the uncontrollably horny state that I found myself in. I'd been waking up in this condition every morning for the past ten days.

Gary was the cause of it all. I watched him for a moment. He was sleeping quietly, his golden hair gleaming in the morning sun that slanted through the wall-to-wall windows of my Beverly Hills bedroom. His face was boyishly handsome. I looked at him, and wanted him. I wanted his mouth against mine, his body pressing onto mine, his cock deep inside me.

That's the way it was when I first met him a couple of weeks ago, on the set of the movie he was starring in. I looked at him, and something about him made me desire him, there and then. It was purely, deliciously physical.

Of course, I wasn't the only woman who found him sexy. Gary was, after all, Hollywood's latest sex symbol. He had starred in a string of suspense movies which had made him the idol of teenage girls all across America.

However, while most of his fans had no hope of getting close to their hero, with my wealth and my friends in the movie business it had been no problem for me to arrange a meeting. And then, I'm pleased to say, it turned out that Gary felt exactly the same kind of powerful lust for me that I felt for him. Result: a passionate affair which kept us in bed for most of the time we were in each other's company. He spent the days making his movie, and the nights making me.

I glanced out the window. Birds were singing outside, and the branches of the peach tree by the swimming pool were rocking to and fro in a slight breeze. The California sun was a powerful, mellow gold.

I yawned and stretched and ran my hands lightly over the soft skin of my stomach, my fingers gradually moving down into the curls of my pubic hair. I couldn't resist touching myself. I spread my labes with two fingers of my left hand, and let the forefinger of my right hand move ever so lightly across my clitoris.

I let out my breath in a long, contented sigh, then stroked myself again. This was what I needed so much—and yet, of course, it only made me feel sexier. I looked at Gary again, and once again I imagined his cock inside me. Just thinking about it made me wet.

I stole a glance at the alarm clock. The time was 6:30. We had half an hour before Gary had to get up and go to the studio. I rolled closer to him.

I ran my fingers through the blond curly hairs of his chest, and traced the muscular rounded shape of his shoulder. I touched the side of his neck, and then his sun-reddened, freckled face. My fingertips delicately ran across his firm, full lips.

Gary stirred in his sleep, but he didn't waken.

I decided there wasn't enough time for this subtle

approach. I wriggled closer to him, pressing the whole length of my body against his, and kissed him hard on the mouth.

His eyes opened sleepily. I continued kissing him, and wriggled against him so that my plump, heavy breasts rubbed across his chest. Gradually he began to respond: His mouth opened under mine, our tongues touched, and then he reached for me and his strong arms pulled me to him. I felt down between his legs and found that his cock was already erect.

"Don't you ever get enough?" he murmured, breaking the kiss. He wasn't complaining, though. He smiled at me fondly as he said it.

"Not yet, not from you," I answered him. "And by the feel of it," I said, squeezing his cock, "you need it just as much as I do."

"Christina, you're wearing me out."

I went on playing with his cock, stroking my fingers along the underside and then tickling it just under its head. "You seem to have some strength left," I told him.

He groaned softly. "I just can't *resist* you," he said. And then he pushed me over onto my back and rolled on top of me in one quick, decisive movement. Each of his wide, capable hands gripped me just above the elbow, holding me down on the bed. I felt my breathing quicken; I loved it when he made me feel helpless like this. He bent his head and kissed me hard, but with a trace of gentleness behind the angry passion.

"I need it, Gary," I whispered to him, as he moved his lips across my cheek, and then down to the side of my neck. "I need it so badly." And it was true. Despite all my sophistication, despite all my experiences with so many men, there was something about him that made me as helplessly horny as a teenager. In fact I almost resented the power he had over me sexually—except that I could see he was just as much under my spell as I was under his. And it felt *so* good!

His cock pushed between my thighs. I felt it, hard and hot, just inches away from my cunt. I opened my legs to him, and he moved up till the head of his cock was probing tantalizingly at my labes.

"Is that what you need, Christina?" he whispered. He nipped at the skin of my neck, just below my ear, and sent shivers running down that side of my body. He jerked his hips, and his cock pushed up, almost into my vagina. "That's what you need?" he repeated.

"Yes. Oh, you know it is!"

He loved to tease me, and make me say how much I wanted him to fuck me. It turned him on more than anything. Maybe it was his actor's ego, always needing to know how much his audience wanted him.

He rubbed his body over mine. He was muscular, but not heavy; tall, but no giant. He brushed his lips fleetingly across mine, and wriggled his hips some more, still tantalizing me with the end of his cock. "Do you want it enough to ask for it, Chris?" he murmured to me.

I felt my breath coming in quick, shallow gasps. I nodded.

"Ask for it, then," he told me. He reached down, took hold of his cock, and rubbed it up and down along the wetness, across my clitoris, then barely into my vagina.

"Fuck me, Gary," I whispered. I looked up at his face as I spoke, and saw how much the words aroused him. "Please fuck me," I said. "I beg you to fuck me."

The muscles knotted in his shoulders and neck. I could sense how much he wanted me. He couldn't resist that need. He guided his cock into me, and then forced it deep, deep inside.

He let himself fall on top of me then, and his hips ground against mine. He kissed me long and deep, pushing his tongue between my lips so that I felt he was invading my mouth, just as he was invading my cunt, and I was totally possessed by him. My body started twisting and jerking completely out of control, and soon, overwhelmed by the torrents of erotic sensations coursing through me, I came. I freed my mouth from his and moaned with fulfillment, and then, as I saw Gary hesitate, I pleaded, "Don't stop! Don't stop, I need more!"

He grinned and held me tightly, then went on fucking me, taking me with long, deliberate strokes now, his cock probing so deep that I felt as if he were reaching to the very core of my soul. Then he rolled over so that we were lying on our sides, and he reached down and found my clitoris and started rubbing it insistently, in rhythm with the upward thrusts of his hips.

He propped himself up with his other arm so that he could look down at me and observe the effects of what he was doing. "Are you going to come again for me, Chris?" he whispered. He forced his cock in deeply, making me gasp and shiver. "*Are* you?"

"I don't know." I swallowed hard. The sensations were building again, and I felt quite helpless to resist. "I don't—oh!" I let out the involuntary cry as he suddenly began moving much faster, thrusting into me in a series of sudden, angry, passionate movements, his finger still pressing on my wet, swollen clitoris.

I clenched my fists and arched my back, closing my eyes as the sensations overwhelmed me.

"Come, Chris," I heard him saying to me. "I want to watch you come again. *Come!*"

It was a command, and I couldn't have refused it even if I had wanted to. I heard myself moaning and shouting, making all kinds of embarrassing, passionate, unladylike sounds. I felt a torrent of sensations leading to pure, ecstatic fulfillment. And then the sudden, clenching spasms died away and I was left in a relaxed, languorous, contented state of bliss, warm and sated. I opened my eyes and found him still looking at my face.

"You're beautiful," he told me. He kissed me, more gently than before, though I could still feel how aroused he was. He stroked my cheek. "Beautiful."

I shook my long blond hair away from my face, knowing how he liked to see it spread out across the pillow. I smiled at him, feeling ridiculously shy.

"My turn, now," he said softly, beginning to move his cock in me again. He pushed himself up and rolled so that once again he was on top of me. I looked up at him, his face so handsome in the golden morning sun, and I couldn't help thinking of all the teenage girls who would have given almost anything to be in my place, in bed with Gary. But it was *me* he wanted, *me* he found so irresistible. When I thought about that, it was like an aphrodisiac.

He braced himself with his arms stretched out on either side of my shoulders. I saw his jaw muscles clench as he started fucking me. I heard his breathing. I saw his forehead grow damp with perspiration.

The bed shook and rocked with the force of his thrusts. I opened my legs wide and cupped my breasts in my hands, holding them up to him. Then he bent his head downward and closed his lips around first one nipple, then the other, sucking and tonguing them and letting me feel just the edge of his teeth, while he went on fucking me, never faltering in the quick, urgent rhythm.

And then he came, gasping and groaning, his cock all the way inside me. He slowly let himself fall down upon me, and I felt the tension ebb out of him. I hugged him, loving the feel of him and the smell of him. I kissed his face. I ran my fingers through his hair. He lay with his eyes closed for a moment, and then rolled off me. "I don't know how you do it, Chris," he said.

"Do what?"

"Get me so turned on."

"It's mutual, Gary," I told him. "I've been constantly horny since the day I met you." Which was true.

He just laughed. He ran his hands over my breasts, then touched my belly and my thighs, his finger finally exploring me where I was wet with my own juices and his semen. "I'd like to stay here in bed with you all day," he murmured. "Wish to hell I didn't have to go and work on that dumb movie."

"But you enjoy your work, Gary."

"I enjoy you more." He kissed me, and then, reluctantly, he got out of bed. "Any chance of some scrambled eggs and coffee?"

If he'd been almost any other man I'd have told him to make his own breakfast. But for Gary, I would do it. While he showered, I put on my robe and went into the kitchen.

About twenty minutes later I was sitting watching him finish his meal. He was dressed casually in jeans and a checked shirt that was open at the neck, revealing just a glimpse of the hairs on his chest. He looked just like one of his own publicity photographs.

He finished his coffee and stood up. "Thanks, Christina." He looked down at me. My chiffon robe was belted loosely; when I moved my shoulders it opened almost to the waist, revealing the tanned, rounded inner sides of my breasts. I saw Gary look down, just as I had intended him to. Then he stepped closer to me. He slid both hands down inside my robe and squeezed both my breasts. "I *still* can't keep my hands off you," he said.

He started rubbing his thumbs in little circles over my nipples. Then he bent down and kissed me, long and hard on the mouth.

I let him enjoy himself for a moment, and then I pulled away. "Too bad you have to go now," I told him teasingly. "I guess you'll have to wait till tonight."

"Tonight, eh?" He stared at my face, then at my body. He laughed and shook his head. "All right, tonight. I'll call you from the set, Chris, and we'll meet for dinner. Okay?"

"Sure," I told him, congratulating myself for having made myself irresistible to him.

I walked him to the door. "See you later," I said. Then I watched him drive away, down the winding road that descended through lush vegetation to the San Fernando Valley.

Less than an hour later, I was still dressed only in my robe, finishing my own breakfast, when the front door bell rang.

I frowned, wondering who would visit me so early. I was not a morning person, and all my friends knew that. As I went to the door, I started feeling angry with whoever had come to disturb my day.

I opened the door. Standing outside was a woman I'd never seen before. She was short and slightly plump, with a round, pink face and wire-framed glasses. Her hair was pulled back in a bun. She looked like somebody's aunt. She stared up at me intently, as if she were examining me. Then she gave me a strange, wide smile, the kind of smile I'd seen on the faces of Jesus freaks. "Miss van Bell," she said. She had a deep voice for a woman, and a foreign accent. "So lucky you're home. I hope you can help me."

"What do you want?" I stood so that I blocked the doorway. If this woman was selling some kind of religion, I wasn't buying.

"My name is Helen Stanowski," she went on. She sounded German, or maybe Scandinavian—I couldn't pin it down. "I'm sorry to disturb you so early, but it's an emergency."

I frowned. "What are you talking about? How do you know who I am?"

"Saw your name on the mailbox. You see, my husband and I just moved into a house a little way up the hill. He was taken ill during the night, and I'm afraid it may be serious. We don't have a phone installed yet, so I came to see if I could use yours, to call a doctor."

She said it all with the same fixed smile, and her eyes kept studying my face. I couldn't figure her at all. There was something about her that gave me the creeps—but on the other hand, I knew there'd been an empty house up the hill, and I'd heard some people had moved into it. And if there really was an emergency, as she said, I couldn't turn her away just because I didn't like her face.

"Sure, you can use my phone," I said reluctantly. "Come in." I stepped to one side.

She bustled past me. "Thank you. A lovely house you have here. Delightful." She moved faster than I had expected; by the time I'd closed the front door and turned around, she was heading down the hall toward the bedrooms.

"You can use the phone in the kitchen," I called after her.

There was no reply.

I cursed silently and went after the woman. "Did you hear me, Mrs. . . . ?" What was her name? "There's a phone in the kitchen. Back this way."

"And you have all this to yourself," I heard her say, completely ignoring me, as she stuck her head into first one room and then the next.

I shook my head in disbelief. The lady was a kook. I

went after her and grabbed her arm. "*This* way," I said, leading her back along the hallway.

She followed me obediently. "Of course, of course. Silly of me. You don't get lonely, in such a big house?"

"I'm a big girl. I can look after myself."

"Yes, I see," the little dumpy woman said. "And that's the living room through there? And here's the kitchen. Ah, yes."

"There's the phone." I pointed her toward it, and stood in the doorway. "If this is a real emergency, I should think you ought to call a doctor right away."

"Indeed." She nodded, but she didn't go over to the phone. She turned and stared at me again.

For the first time, I started feeling uneasy. It was one thing to deal with a woman who was a little kooky. It was another thing to realize she could be quite crazy, and even dangerous. When she gave me that blissed-out smile again, I instinctively closed my robe more tightly around myself and took a step backward. "So are you going to make the call or not?" I asked, realizing my voice was becoming shrill.

"It won't be necessary." She laughed, and it was a weird, manic sound. "I just told you a little story. All I wanted was to come and meet you and give you a present, Miss van Bell." She took a step toward me.

I decided the woman was totally bananas. Christ, I thought, what should I do? Get her out of the house. Humor her. "A present, for me? That's nice," I said unconvincingly. I took another step back. "Actually I'm kind of busy right now, and—"

"But I *insist*." She reached in her handbag and took something out. Then she came toward me.

It happened very quickly. She pointed the thing at my face. There was a hissing noise.

I took a breath and choked, then realized the woman had sprayed something at me—some kind of aerosol.

Mace, or something. I gasped. My lungs felt on fire. Then a wave of dizziness swept over me.

I tried to hold onto the wall for support. I blinked and saw a double image of the woman standing back, watching me. She wasn't smiling anymore. Her eyes were hard and bright, like some predatory bird's eyes.

"Just relax, Miss van Bell," I heard her saying from a long way off. "We'll take care of you."

I felt myself falling, unable to control my muscles. But my mind was still working, and I realized then that this had to be a kidnapping. She would have seen Gary leave the house. She would have waited to make sure Gary wasn't coming back. Then the phone-call story, and then she'd made sure there was no one else here with me, in any of the rooms. . . .

I tried to shout for help, but I couldn't make a sound. Even breathing was becoming an effort. My pulse was thudding in my ears, and I began to feel terrified that the drug she'd sprayed at me was going to kill me. Once again I tried to shout, but my mouth wouldn't open, and then there was a prick in my arm, and I passed out completely.

CHAPTER TWO

As I regained consciousness I heard the distant sound of surf. Somewhere, waves were breaking in a steady rhythm. At the same time, my head was throbbing with pain. I groaned and tried to turn over, but something or someone was holding me by the wrists.

With an effort I managed to open my eyes. I was lying on my back on a big, soft bed, and for a moment I thought it might be my own bed in my own home. But no; this bed had an old-fashioned brass frame, and it was in a big, bare room with wide windows that overlooked a totally deserted beach. The sun was setting over the ocean, as the waves rolled in, and I realized with dismay that I must have been unconscious for the whole of the day, or maybe even longer.

I winced. The pain in my head made me close my eyes again. I tried to swallow and found that my throat was dry. My pulse beating quickly, I took several deep breaths to try to stop myself from panicking.

I heard a door open and close, and then I heard footsteps coming toward me across thick carpeting. Once again I opened my eyes. I saw the person walking toward me where I lay on the bed, and she was the same short, round-faced little woman who had abducted me from my home. Her eyes gleamed behind her wire-framed glasses as she looked at me. She smiled her weird, vacant smile.

I tried instinctively to pull back from her. That was when I realized that my wrists had been tightly tied to the brass bed frame. I was helpless.

"So you're awake, my dear Miss van Bell," the woman was saying. She studied my nakedness for a moment. Then she sat down beside me on the bed and laid her hand on my forehead. "How are you feeling?"

I flinched from her touch. I tugged futilely at the nylon rope binding my wrists. "What . . . the hell is going on?" I asked, my voice trembling with a mixture of fear and anger.

"Calm yourself, Miss van Bell." She patted me on my bare shoulder. Then she pressed her fingers against the side of my neck.

"No!" I screamed, trying to pull away. For a moment I imagined the woman was going to strangle me. Something about her touch freaked me out completely.

"Hold still, dear." Her voice was very businesslike. "I just want to take your pulse." And then she grabbed a hank of my long, golden hair in her left hand and tightened her grip till I cried out. She held my head this way, making it impossible for me to move, till she'd finished taking my pulse at the artery at the side of my neck. Then she released me.

"You see, Miss van Bell," she told me, "it's so much easier if you cooperate."

I closed my eyes and felt like breaking down and crying. I was so helpless and vulnerable; I didn't even know where I was. "What do you want?" I blurted out. "How much money?"

"Money?" The woman laughed mockingly. It was an ugly sound, very brittle and manic. "My dear, money is the least of our concerns."

There was something about the way she said this, in her rather deep voice and her foreign accent, that sent a chill through me. "Then why did you kidnap me?" I stammered. "If you don't want my money—"

She reached out and ran her fingers down the side of my cheek. Then she cupped her hand around my left breast and held it for a moment. I squirmed under her touch. The woman was a lesbian, I was certain of that much. "We want *you*, my dear Christina. That's why we chose you. Not for your money. For your unique and lovely self. That's all."

"Jesus Christ," I muttered. I felt as if I were sinking deeper and deeper, further and further away from the real world and everyday life. This woman was insane; she was part of some kind of California cult. Satanists, murderers, it could be anything. I cursed myself for ever having let her into my home. I had always meant to take precautions against a kidnap attempt. But I'd never actually done anything to safeguard myself, and now I was paying the penalty. A much higher penalty, perhaps, than I had ever imagined.

"Well, you've certainly recovered satisfactorily from the sedative we gave you," the woman said. She stood up and put her hands on her hips, once again surveying my nakedness.

I tried to pull my knees up so that I would feel less exposed and vulnerable, but I discovered that my ankles had been tied to the frame at the foot of the bed. The ropes were not as tight as the ropes that held my wrists, but they still effectively prevented me from concealing myself. "What happened to my robe?" I asked. "And my slippers." My voice sounded plaintive, almost like a whimper. I hated the way this crazy woman had taken away my initiative and my strength.

"All your things were destroyed," she said matter-of-factly. "Including your jewelry, Miss van Bell."

"What?" I turned my head, rubbing my face against the bed to try to feel whether I was still wearing my pearl earrings. No—they were gone. I flexed my fingers and discovered that my jade signet ring was also missing.

"We didn't want any links with your former life. You have to make a completely fresh start here, Miss van Bell."

For some reason this upset me more than anything else that had happened. They had left me with nothing, absolutely nothing. "You—you'll pay," I gasped. "I'll make you pay." But my voice sounded frail and unconvincing, and the woman just smiled her thin, crazy smile, as if my hopelessness turned her on in some perverted way.

I turned my head and stared out the window at the ocean. The view became blurred as I felt the last of my strength ebbing away, and I began crying.

Somewhere behind me I heard the woman walk across the room, open a door, and walk out, leaving me alone.

For a while I slipped back into unconsciousness. Maybe I fainted; it was hard to tell. I was still very groggy from the drug that the woman had originally given me.

When I next awoke, I once more heard the sound of the waves coming faintly through the thick glass of the windows. But I could no longer see anything outside. It had grown completely dark.

Someone had turned on a small table lamp in the room where I lay. I blinked and looked around. My head was no longer so painful, and I felt a little stronger than before.

Once again the woman was standing looking down at my naked body, but this time she had someone with her, standing beside her. He was a man in his forties, and he looked very much like her, with the same round, fleshy face and the same steel-framed glasses. His clothes were baggy and shapeless, and he stood with a slight stoop, as if he had no awareness of his body and didn't care how he looked. He was partially bald.

"This is my brother Carl," the woman said. "He's an extremely brilliant chemist. It was he who synthesized the sedative we administered to you, Miss van Bell." She sounded as if she was expecting me to congratulate him on his achievement.

"My own name is Helen, as you may remember," the woman ran on. "Helen Stanowski. I was trained as a doctor, myself." She turned to her brother. "You see, Carl, Miss van Bell was an ideal choice."

The slightly plump little man studied me with sharp, clear blue eyes. He took a step closer, sat down on the side of the bed, and without any warning ran his right hand over my belly and down my thighs, feeling me as if I were a farm animal up for auction. Then he took hold of one of my breasts and squeezed it slowly, watching my face.

I let out a cry of surprise and dismay and tried to pull away from him. But I was still tied hand and foot, and there was nothing I could do. Suddenly I felt myself getting angry. "What the hell *is* this?" I shouted. "Christ, who *are* you people? You bastard—"

"You are in no position to call names," the little man interrupted. His accent was much heavier than his sister's. It sounded Germanic. He kept his hand on my breast, as if to make it clear to me that he could do whatever he wanted with me, and if I fought him or swore at him this would only make things worse.

With difficulty, I fought back my anger. I told myself that it would make much more sense to be submissive, at least until I had figured out more about what was going on. There was no point in trying to fight them till I had some chance of winning.

Carl saw the change in me as I stopped struggling and lay meekly on the bed. He smiled the same thin smile that I had already come to know and detest on the face of his sister, Helen. "Good," he said. He stood up. "Ideal, I agree," he said to the woman still standing beside him. Then he turned back toward me. "We will release you, Miss van Bell, in just a moment. It is almost time for you to meet Josef."

"What?" I looked from one of them to the other. "Look, I don't want to meet anyone. I just want to go home. Tell me how much it'll take. I'll give you the money. Whatever you want."

The two of them looked at each other and smiled in a kind of conspiratorial way. Then Helen Stanowski looked down at me. "You will not be going home, Miss van Bell. Not now, maybe never. Your money is no interest. Now, we will untie you, but you must realize, if you struggle we will have to sedate you again. Worse still, we will have to teach you to behave yourself, and that will be *painful*." A strange, dreamy look came into her eyes as she said that last word. I could see that making things *painful* for me wouldn't bother her at all. In fact, she probably hoped I would make it necessary.

"So behave," Carl chimed in. He started loosening the rope that secured my left wrist. "Be good girl. Yes?"

"All right," I said in a small voice. I still felt weak from the drug, and there was obviously no way I was going to overpower the pair of them. Even if I could, there would be other people to cope with. I was sure of that.

So I lay still as they released my hands and feet. My muscles were stiff and cramped; it took me a few minutes to exercise some life back into them. Then, with an effort, I sat up on the edge of the bed.

For the first time I got a good look at the room I was in. It contained no furniture except the bed and a small table where the lamp was standing. The walls were painted off-white. There was a deep-pile beige carpet covering the whole of the floor. That was all.

"Come, Miss Christina van Bell." Carl took my wrist in his hand. "We go meet Josef." He pronounced it as if it were *Yosif*.

I held back. "Can't I have some clothes?" I hated the way my nakedness made me feel so vulnerable. And I hated the way both these weirdos kept staring at me.

"No, no clothes." Carl laughed. He looked at my tits. Then, once again, he ran his hands over me. "We have to keep you naked, yes."

It took all my self-control to stand there and let him touch me, when what I wanted was to jam my knee into his crotch and attack his face with my fingernails.

Helen Stanowski opened the door. "Come, Miss van Bell. With us."

Obediently, I did as she said.

CHAPTER THREE

Helen and Carl Stanowski led me along a windowless passageway to a heavy, oak-paneled door. Carl knocked and waited till there was a faint acknowledgment from within. Then he turned the big brass handle and swung the door open.

I found myself in a room that was easily a hundred feet long. Like the room in which I had awoken, it was almost bare of furniture. The floor was covered in an unbroken expanse of thick-pile carpet, in a rich, deep shade of purple. This extended up a series of steps at the far end of the room, where a massive chair, like a throne, stood in the center of a platform. A man was reclining there, watching me.

"Go and present yourself to him," Helen Stanowski instructed me. She nudged me forward.

The thick carpet was sensuous and soft under my feet. The room was totally without windows, I realized as I stepped forward. And the lighting was so dim that I could barely make out the man in the big chair.

I've seen my share of palatial residences. My own home in Beverly Hills is lavish and impressive. But something about this almost totally bare, windowless room was intimidating.

I glanced over my shoulder and saw that the Stanowskis were still standing by the door, as if they were not allowed to proceed any farther without special permission. Then I continued walking toward the man in the chair. I tried to move with more assurance than I actually felt. The room was totally silent, so that the noise of my own breathing and my rapid heartbeats was loud in my ears.

I hesitated when I reached the first of the carpeted steps up to the dais. The man in the chair slowly got to his feet. He had thick black hair, just long enough to cover his ears. He had a black beard, meticulously trimmed, outlining the contours of his heavy, square jaw. His shoulders were very broad, almost like those of a weight lifter, outlined by a black silk shirt which he wore unbuttoned to his waist, exposing a wide and well-tanned chest almost devoid of body hair. He was wearing black silk pants, Chinese-wrestler style, to match the shirt. He was perhaps six feet two inches tall, an elegant figure, but at the same time somehow streetwise and tough. He watched me steadily, leaving me in no doubt that he was in charge here.

"Christina van Bell," he said slowly, coolly examining first my face and then my body. He grinned unexpectedly, showing his perfect, pure white teeth. "Step up and join me," he said, in a deep, rich voice which almost sounded welcoming. "Make yourself comfortable."

I started up the three steps. I looked around uncertainly; there was nowhere for me to sit.

"On the floor," he told me, with a new edge to his voice which wasn't welcoming at all. "Sit." And he pointed at the floor just in front of his feet.

For a moment I marveled at his arrogance. I wondered what he would do if I defied him. I sensed pent-up violence in him. I was sure he would have no compunction about hitting or hurting me. And this wasn't the moment to stage a confrontation. So I did as he told me. But I moved slowly, taking my time. And I continued to return his steady stare, as if I believed I could challenge his authority.

"Good," he said softly, after a moment. "You are arrogant. I like that." He sat back in his enormous chair and folded his arms, still surveying me as if I were a new playything which had just been delivered to him. "Welcome to my community, Christina," he went on. "My name is Josef."

"Community?" I said blankly.

"Indeed." He reached across to an antique table beside the chair and picked up a large leather-bound book. He threw it down onto the floor beside me. "Open it," he told me.

I picked up the book and started leafing through it. It was a deluxe photo album. On each page was a ten-by-eight color picture. Each picture showed a young man or woman in close-up. They were all good-looking, all healthy, tanned, and smiling. I recognized a couple of well-known faces: a television actress, a cross-country skiing champion. Then I reached the last page and stopped in surprise. On that page was a picture of me.

I looked up at Josef. He studied my expression as if it were mildly amusing to him. Then he put out his hand and dumbly I handed the book back to him. "The people you see here are the new members of my community," he said. "Including you. In fact, you are the last one to join us. The others are already here."

Slowly I realized what he meant. I stared at him. "You mean you've kidnapped all those people and brought them here?"

"Of course. You have already seen how easy it was to bring *you* here. It was very little trouble, with the assistance of my friends." He inclined his head toward Helen and Carl Stanowski, still standing patiently by the door.

"But why?" I blurted out.

He shrugged. "A community, as I say. One which will exist without any interference from the outside world. Totally private, and organized along lines of my devising. *My* utopia, Christina, with permanent residents such as yourself, who will try their hardest to please me." He laughed. "Don't you think that sounds wonderful? Don't you think that's the greatest fantasy you ever heard? And now it's *all coming true*." His eyes widened slightly as he spoke, and his face took on the look of a fanatic.

I stared at him with horrified fascination. He was so amazingly handsome and had so much charisma, I felt the force of his personality. Under normal circumstances, I would have found him a very attractive man, except for the fact that he was obviously insane. For a moment I wondered what had driven him to this scheme. Had a woman rejected him for some reason when he was younger? It seemed unlikely. Did he simply enjoy controlling other people?

I shook my head slowly. "It's too grandiose," I said. "Anything as big as this is going to be discovered. It won't work." I tried to speak with quiet conviction, to see whether he had any doubts about the plan himself. I wanted to find the slightest evidence of weakness in him. If there was any weakness there, maybe I could somehow exploit it.

But he merely laughed and gestured scornfully. "What do you know about us?" he said. "What could you possibly know? You, with your protected life, your house in Beverly Hills, your penthouse in Manhattan, your villa on the Côte d'Azur—yes, I have investigated your life, I know all about you. You lead a life insulated from the cruelties and hardships and dangers of the world. Expensive cars and clothes, men fawning over you, no challenges, no risks." He sounded as if he were condemning this vision of luxury, and yet at the same time I suspected he was envying it. Maybe that was his motivation—to get even with people who were rich.

Again he reached across to the table beside him, picked up something white and formless made of cloth, and tossed it down to me. Instinctively I caught it. I held it up and saw that it was a leotard.

"Put it on," he instructed. "Now. While I watch you."

Once again I debated whether to defy him. Once again I realized that there was no advantage in doing so. I stood up, still trying to move with poise and self-possession. I stepped into the leotard and started pulling it up over my body.

"Closer," he told me. He leaned forward. "And don't turn away." His eyes were studying me, catching every little movement. Somehow I felt more self-conscious and more abused than if he had been staring at my total nudity. The garment was very tight-fitting, and I had to squirm and wriggle as I pulled it over my skin. It was as skimpy and as inviting as a Playboy bunny costume. I realized he was making me exhibit myself to him, whether I liked it or not.

"Move more slowly," he told me as I pulled the leotard up over my breasts. I had to squash them down inside it. The nipples showed plainly through the thin white fabric. Josef grinned. "Very nice," he murmured.

I clenched my fists and turned away, trembling with frustrated anger at him for making me degrade myself in front of him.

He reached out quickly and grabbed my wrist in his hand. His grip was sudden and strong. "Did I give you permission to turn away from me?" he asked. His voice was loud and sharp. "*Did I?* Kneel down on the floor. Where you were before. Go on."

He glared at me, waiting for me to obey him.

My breath was coming in quick, shallow gasps. I clenched my fists till my nails dug painfully into my palms. I stared back at him in open defiance.

His grip tightened on my wrist. "Christina," he said, and suddenly his voice was soft but somehow much more frightening. "You do realize that no one knows where you are, and I could do anything I like to you— anything at all—right here and now. You do realize that?"

A dozen different angry images flashed through my head. I imagined kicking him in the face, then grabbing his balls and squeezing them till he started crying for mercy. I imagined hurling him through a window and watching him plummet twenty stories down to a street. But my imagination didn't have the power to change anything. He was right: I was at his mercy. Still trembling with suppressed emotion, I slowly knelt down on the floor at his feet.

He reached out and patted my hair. "Very good. Very good, Christina. But I can see that a spirited young woman like you is going to have trouble learning to be obedient. So I should explain to you that we have already provided a kind of incentive for you. Look at the skin of your left arm, just inside your elbow. Yes, look there. Tell me what you find."

Reluctantly, I did as he told me. To my surprise I found a little spot of congealed blood. "A pinprick," I said.

"An injection," he corrected me. "A clever idea of Carl's. While you were unconscious we dosed you with a new drug that he's invented."

A new and horrible fear settled in my stomach, replacing the anger I had felt a moment previously. I remembered falling unconscious in my home, when Helen Stanowski had used the aerosol spray on me. The last thing I had felt before blacking out had been a hypodermic needle.

"I don't pretend to know exactly how it works," Josef added, "but you know, don't you, that the blood transports oxygen to the brain? Without that, you die quite quickly. Carl tells me this new drug of his replaces the body's own system for bonding the oxygen to the blood cells, or something like that. So you now need the drug for your body to continue functioning normally. But the drug gets excreted via the kidneys, so you have to have another dose of it every day. Unless you get your daily dose, you die. Naturally, we have the only supply. And because it's a new invention, there's no antidote." He sat back in his big chair. "Remember this, Christina, whenever you feel rebellious, remember how much you need us to care for you." Once again he patted my head, not in a fatherly fashion, but like the cruel owner of a new pet.

I felt numb. There was nothing I could say. Assuming that what he had told me was true, I was totally helpless. The enormity of it was too overwhelming. My mind couldn't grasp it.

He reached down and squeezed my breast through the thin leotard. I realized with horror that he could do anything to me now, and I wouldn't be able to even complain, let alone try to resist.

"Don't worry, Christina," he said. His deep voice was gentle now, almost soothing. "You'll be safe here. I'll take care of you, so long as you continue to please me." His grip tightened. He pinched my nipple between his finger and thumb, not enough to hurt, but enough to remind me of his strength and his power over me. "You *will* please me, won't you? And my friends, too."

"I . . . will please you," I said with difficulty.

"Good. Just one more thing. In the future, whenever

you speak to me, you will call me 'master.' I think you'd better make sure you can do that, right now. Repeat what you just said, bearing this in mind.''

The words almost stuck in my throat. But somehow I managed to say, ''I will please you. Master.''

''Good.'' He let go of my breast and stood up. ''Of course, at this point you are saying it under duress, because you are afraid. But as time passes you will reach the point where you, and all my other guests, will truly *want* to serve and please me.'' His tone was now brusque and businesslike. He took hold of my arm and pulled me quickly up and onto my feet. He was terrifyingly strong.

''Go and meet the rest of them,'' he said. ''I have no further use for you, for now. Go on.'' He pushed me suddenly, and I fell down the steps from the dais and landed on the floor below.

He stood staring at me, his hands on his hips, his legs spread wide apart. Towering over me, he looked like an unassailable giant.

I picked myself up, shaken, bruised, terrified, and furious at the way he had abused me. I walked away from him, back to Carl Stanowski and his sister, Helen, where they were waiting to escort me out of the room.

CHAPTER FOUR

They led me down a flight of stairs to a basement door fitted with a big combination lock. Helen Stanowski held my arm while Carl worked the lock, hiding it from me so that I was unable to see the figures as he turned the dial.

"It's time you met your companions, Christina," Helen told me matter-of-factly. I hardly heard her; I was still livid after my meeting with Josef. In my mind I was running through all the ways in which I should have defied him or tried to fight back. And yet I knew there was nothing I could have done. If he was telling the truth about the drug they'd given me, I was truly under their control.

Carl opened the door and stepped back. Helen pushed me through into the room that lay beyond. "Make yourself at home," she called after me. Then they slammed the door behind me, leaving me there.

I found myself in a long, wide, low-ceilinged place furnished with wall-to-wall carpet, pillow couches, and a couple of long, low tables. There were no windows. Spotlights recessed into the ceiling cast a uniform light over the scene.

Three men and three women were sitting there. I realized that their faces were familiar: I had seen them all in the photo album Josef had shown me. These were his "guests"—my fellow members of his commune, or whatever he chose to call it. I looked at them. They looked at me.

Finally one of the men stood up. He was wearing nothing more than a pair of boxer shorts, and I noticed that the other two men were fitted out in the same way, while the women were in tight leotards like the one I had been given. Presumably everyone had gone through the same initiation ceremony I had just experienced, and had had all clothes and possessions taken away.

"My name's Robert French," said the guy who had stood up. He stepped toward me and put out his hand. Automatically, I shook it.

"Christina van Bell," I told him, hearing myself say the words as if I were somewhere else watching myself in the scene. I didn't want to believe I was really down in that basement, locked in with those people, without any way of escaping.

"Welcome to our luxury jailhouse," said Robert French. His face twisted into a quick, cynical smile. He let go of my hand and gestured awkwardly. "Ample room for us all, full kitchen facilities, no shortage of food." His voice was a little too loud, and all his movements were tense and clumsy. I figured the confinement was getting to him, probably more than he would have liked to admit. "I was the first one they brought here," he went on. "Stuck in this hole for more than a week now. Let me introduce you to the others."

Suddenly I found myself feeling weak and dizzy. I realized I was in no shape to meet all six of them and try to make conversation. I was experiencing a delayed reaction to the scene with Josef, and I needed a chance to absorb all that had happened. "I'm—a little shaky right now," I told French. "If you'll excuse me"—I forced a smile in the direction of the rest of the prisoners—"I think I'd better sit down for a minute and get myself together." I took a couple of steps to the nearest couch and sank onto it.

"Perhaps you'd like a drink of water? Or something to eat?" French asked, looking at me.

"Yes. That would be good." I realized how empty my stomach was, which was another reason I was feeling faint.

"Fine," said French. "Wait right there. They give us everything we need—oh, everything," he said sarcastically. He walked away to the kitchen area.

I sat quietly for a moment, closing my eyes and trying to make myself relax. Then I felt a hand on my shoulder. I looked up and saw one of the women standing over me, her head tilted to one side inquiringly. She had dark brown wavy hair, an oval face, hazel eyes. She was pretty, and she had a look of sharp intelligence. She was watching me with a mixture of shrewdness and compassion. "Don't worry," she told me in a gentle, reassuring voice. "Take it a minute at a time. And remember that, so far, none of us has been harmed in any way."

There was something about her low-key approach that made me feel much better. I instantly decided that I liked this woman, and could trust her. "Thanks," I said, forcing a smile.

"My name's Alexandra Jones," she told me.

"Christina van Bell," I said, shaking her hand.

"Do you want me to leave you alone for a little while?" she asked.

I shook my head no. I realized she would be easy to talk to, unlike Robert French, who was so much on edge it had made me tense just listening to him introduce himself. "Sit down," I told Alexandra.

She joined me on the couch. "I guess you'd like to know where you are and what's been happening here," she said. She had a girlish manner, almost like a teenager, but when I looked at her closely, I realized she had to be in her late twenties. And her eyes were more intense than her easygoing manner suggested.

"Yes, I'd like to know that, very much," I agreed.

"Well, we don't know where we are," she said. "Each one of us was kidnapped, drugged, and woke up here maybe six or eight hours later. You too, I expect."

I nodded. "Right."

"And each of us had a welcome-to-my-world interview with the guy who calls himself Josef," she went on.

"Yeah. He wasn't exactly a pussycat."

"Did he hurt you, Christina?" She was watching me carefully.

"Well, no," I admitted. "Just made it clear who's in control, I guess."

Alexandra nodded. "Our experience, precisely. Each one of us went through his initiation procedure, was brought down here, and then—nothing."

I frowned. "What do you mean, nothing?"

"Exactly what I say. They keep us locked in here. A new person arrives each day. The refrigerator is full of food, and we help ourselves. There's a bathroom. That's all. It's boring as hell."

"Those are the facts, all right," said Robert French, returning with a paper cup of water and a sandwich on a paper plate. "For all we know, this is some sort of war on our nerves. Maybe they want to see how long it'll take to drive us crazy." He laughed. It was a harsh, brittle sound. I accepted the food and water from him, and instinctively edged away. I didn't want to end up like him—edgy and desperate.

"Of course, we have time on our side," he went on, in his penetrating voice. "They have to make a move in the end, and then . . . do you realize how few kidnap attempts are ever really successful? They always slip up. Always. Especially when it comes to picking up the ransom money. And I'll tell you, it's going to be a real pleasure to see these bastards in court. A real pleasure. I happen to be a criminal lawyer. In fact, you may have heard of me. A case of mine was written up in the Los Angeles *Times* just a couple of weeks back. I defended some movie people who were implicated in the Laurel Canyon bust. Got them off, all of them."

"Robert," Alexandra interrupted, "Christina probably needs some peace and quiet right now."

He stopped, looking offended. "If that's the way you want it," he said, and turned and walked away. He started pacing up and down the far side of the basement, muttering to himself, his hands clasped behind his back.

"He can't accept being confined in here," Alexandra whispered to me. "He's used to being in control. All he can talk about is getting back at Josef and the Stanowskis. It drives him crazy that there's nothing he can do to help himself or the rest of us."

"I see." I looked at the sandwich he had brought me. It had ham in it. I took a big bite and it tasted good. "So what do you think, Alexandra? What happens next?"

"Well, I guess Josef told you his story about the ideal community he's building."

I nodded.

"So we bide our time till he's assembled all the people in it."

"He said I'm the last person on the list," I told her.

"Oh?" She looked thoughtful, and a little worried. She hesitated for a moment, then took my hand. "Come and meet the rest of us."

Obediently I stood up, realizing she was trying to distract me, and maybe herself as well, from worrying about what might happen to us.

Alexandra led me over to a tall, thin, long-haired guy lying stretched out on the floor with his hands behind his head, as if he were sunbathing on a beach. To judge from his pallid skin, however, he hadn't been in the sun in years. His eyes were half closed and he seemed perfectly relaxed, quietly humming a tune to himself.

"This is Mark Bernstein," Alexandra said.

"Christina van Bell," I introduced myself. Bernstein got up on one elbow, reached out to me, and we shook hands. Suddenly I recognized him—he was a rock musician. I'd seen him on television once.

"Hey, Christina," he said, looking slightly spaced-out. "It's a real pleasure to meet you." Then he let go my hand and lay back down on the floor.

"Being here . . . doesn't seem to bother you very much," I commented.

Bernstein shook his head of messy hair. "Way I figure it, this is the first vacation I've had in three years, and I got about five months' sleep to catch up on. In the meantime I can put down in my head all the songs for my next album. Why sweat it?"

"I see," I said, though really I didn't.

"Each of us has a different way of coping with this situation," Alexandra murmured to me. She led me across the room to a woman reclining alone on one of the couches. "This is Elizabeth Fleming. Elizabeth, meet Christina."

The woman stood up, moving with elaborate grace and poise. She was a striking beauty, her dark eyes framed by a mass of thick black curls, and I recognized her from a recent movie. But age was just beginning to touch her face, and I could see she wasn't going to age gracefully. She was too proud, too pleased with her own elegance, and she despised other people too much. She studied me as if I were an enemy. "A pleasure to meet you, my dear," she said, in a little-girl voice that was meant to be cute but sounded artificial.

"I've enjoyed your movies," I said diplomatically.

"Why, thank you," she answered with a patronizing smile.

Alexandra seemed to realize that I wasn't going to hit it off with Elizabeth. She took my arm. "Let's meet the last two members of the group," she said diplomatically.

These turned out to be a strong, quiet, sun-bronzed man named Michel, and a cute, sexy-looking blonde named Jane. Michel was Swiss; he was the skiing champion I had recognized in the photo album. He seemed uninterested in making small talk with me, or with anyone else for that matter—I guessed that skiing was his whole life, and being imprisoned here was very hard on him.

As for Jane, she was the classic dumb blonde who wanted to get into movies but probably lacked the talent to do so. Her face and body were enough to attract all kinds of attention from producers and casting directors, but not the kind of attention she really wanted. "I guess they picked me because of my looks, not my money," she said, glancing down at her plump, heavy breasts squeezed into a leotard like the one I was wearing myself. She sighed. "It's the story of my life."

So that was the group: Jane, the would-be starlet; Michel, the skiing champion; Elizabeth, the snobbish actress; Mark, the rock musician; Robert, the lawyer; and Alexandra and myself.

"What about you?" I asked Alexandra, retreating with her to a quiet corner. "How do you make a living?"

She smiled to herself. "I get by, any way I can," she said. "I've done secretarial work. I've worked for an escort agency. I did modeling. Hooked up with a guy in the music business for a while; he overdosed on downs and booze one night, and when we got out his will it left me his house, his Rolls-Royce, and most of his money." She shrugged. "That was a year or so ago."

Something about the way she said it made me think she wasn't telling me the whole truth, but I didn't feel like antagonizing her by openly doubting her story. I needed all the friends I could get, and she was the only one I really liked in the group. I decided to change the subject. "What about the drug that we're all supposed to be addicted to?" I asked. "Was that just a story, or is it true?"

"Oh, it's true, all right. Each of us was given a shot when we were originally kidnapped—you too, I guess."

I nodded.

"So now we get one pill a day to maintain the level of medication. The terrible twins—the Stanowskis—come down here and make sure we swallow the tablets."

"The addiction could still be a con," I said. "How can we tell for sure?"

Alexandra nodded. "Yeah, that's how I figured it, too. So one day I pretended to swallow the pill, but kept it under my tongue. I hid it, soon as the Stanowskis were gone. I felt fine for the first few hours, but then I started getting dizzy and began breathing faster and faster. I could tell the oxygen just wasn't getting into my system. I swallowed the pill then, but it took a while to start working, and during that period I fainted. I guess I could have died if I'd delayed taking it any longer. It does what they say it does, Chris. If you don't believe me, just try doing what I did." For the first time, she looked grim and defeated.

"I see." I didn't know what else to say. "So . . . has anyone tried to find a way of breaking out of here?"

Alexandra laughed. "Oh, sure. Robert French went around kicking the walls till his feet hurt. We're below ground level, and the walls are made of concrete, so that's hopeless. Then one night he thought maybe he could break out through the ceiling. They turn the lights out at night, you know. But it seems there's some kind of surveillance system down here, which works even in the dark. They heard or saw Robert banging around and came down here right away, told him he'd get hurt if he tried it again, and gave him some knockout medicine. Anyway, what would we do if we got outside? We're hooked on a drug, and if we don't get our dose every day, we die. It's as simple as that.''

I thought it through. "What if we grabbed Helen Stanowski and threatened to kill her if her brother didn't hand over his supplies of the drug and let us out?"

Alexandra shook her head. "You've been watching too many TV shows, Chris. Kill Helen Stanowski? With what? They've left nothing down here that could be used as a weapon. There are a few plastic knives in the kitchen area. There are no glasses—just paper cups. The bathroom mirror is made of metal. They've thought of everything.''

I sat there, thinking, sure that someone must have missed something. But my thoughts were interrupted.

"I know you're up there, you bastards!" Robert French shouted suddenly, standing at the other side of the room, staring up at the ceiling with his fists clenched. "And I know you can hear me. I'm warning you, if you don't want to rot in jail for the rest of your lives, you better let me out, right now. Do you realize who I am?" He paused, breathing hard. His face was red. "I say, *Do you realize who I am?* I have friends in the district attorney's office. I—" He broke off. "God damn it, you'd better answer me!"

Michel, the skier, got to his feet and walked over. "Calm yourself, Robert," he said quietly, resting his hand on French's shoulder.

"Calm myself?" French said, knocking Michel's hand aside. "You mean sit around like the rest of you, and let those bastards up there do whatever they like to us?" He started pacing up and down. "No, no, there has to be a way out! What do you *want* from us?" he yelled again, glaring up at the ceiling.

There was a moment of silence. And then, to the surprise of us all, a hidden loudspeaker came to life. "No need to shout, Mr. French," the voice said. I realized it was Josef speaking. "I can hear you quite clearly. And believe me, I do regret that the waiting has been so hard on your nerves."

French's face turned an even deeper shade of red. He drew in a breath. "What the hell do you want from us!" French screamed again at the hidden voice.

"Please—don't interrupt me," the voice went on, while Josef presumably watched us all via some hidden camera. "Now that all my guests have been gathered here, there is no need for us to wait any longer. You might say it's time for the *fun* to begin."

There was a click, and the loudspeaker went dead. I looked at Alexandra, and she looked back at me. Even Robert French had become silent.

Then I thought I smelled a strange odor. "Alexandra," I said. "Do you smell something? A scent?"

She looked afraid. "More drugs," she said apprehensively. "They're probably gassing us this time."

CHAPTER FIVE

At first we were all terrified, knowing that the air we were breathing was now loaded with some unknown chemical. Robert French went to the door and started pounding on it and yelling. I lay down and tried to take very small, shallow breaths. But of course any action was hopeless. Nothing could change the fact that we were locked in with nowhere to go.

Several minutes passed. To the surprise of all of us, no one seemed to suffer any ill effects. The smell of the gas grew heavier, but it didn't seem to do us any harm.

In fact, I began to feel a lot more relaxed and much less nervous than before. My muscles gradually loosened, and my skin started to glow with the look of well-being. "This could be some kind of tranquilizer," I said. Even as I spoke, there was a faint smile on my face, as if whatever was happening didn't matter at all.

"Yeah," Robert French growled, still pacing angrily to and fro. But even he seemed to feel less angry and worried now. "They're drugging us to make us complacent and easy to deal with." He shook his head, as if trying to get rid of the mellowness that was gradually softening him.

I looked at Mark, the rock musician. He seemed to have gone to sleep; his eyes were closed and he was breathing gently. One of his hands had fallen idly across his body, down by his crotch. To my surprise I saw a bulge in the boxer shorts he was wearing. If he was asleep, maybe he was having an erotic dream.

I looked at Elizabeth, who was no longer fussing with her manicure. Her face looked a little flushed. She was sitting and staring at Michel, and something in her eyes suggested that she was imagining what kind of lover he would be. And Michel, still as quiet and withdrawn as before, now seemed to be staring at Jane's breasts.

A suspicion began to form in my mind. I turned to Alexandra. "So far as anyone knows," I murmured to her, "there has never, throughout history, been a sure-fire aphrodisiac which would work on both men and women. Am I right?"

She frowned at the odd question. "I've never heard of anything that really worked, no."

"Well, you've heard of one now," I said.

"What do you mean?" And then she realized. "You think this gas has some effect on the sex drive?"

"Don't you feel it?" I was already very conscious of a warm glow enveloping my entire body. My nipples seemed to be getting hard, and there was a moistness in my vagina. No matter how much I tried to bring my thoughts back to my confinement, I could no longer get worried about it. It didn't seem to matter anymore. Nothing mattered except the delicious feelings that were beginning to emanate from my erogenous zones. I thought for a moment of Gary, and wished he were with me at this instant. Just the brief memory of our lovemaking in my bed together, on the morning when I had been kidnapped, sent a wave of sexy feelings tingling through me. I had the sudden urge to masturbate.

"You're right, I do feel aroused," Alexandra whispered. She looked at me in a strange way, then reached out and touched my shoulder. "You're right, Christina. You're absolutely right."

There was something about her slightly parted lips and the way she studied my face so intently, with half-closed eyes, that looked unbearably appealing. I felt a wave of affection for her. "I'm glad you're here," I whispered to her. I stroked her hair. "I feel I can trust you."

Alexandra nodded. "I feel I can trust you too. In fact—" She broke off. She closed her eyes as if trying to cope with something inside herself. "I don't know what's real anymore," she said in a low voice. "Whatever it is we're breathing—" And then despite herself she suddenly giggled. She looked at me again. "I have the most terrible, wicked desire to kiss you, Christina," she told me.

I started giggling myself. I felt like a schoolgirl, giddy and horny and so *very* fond of my new friend. The next thing I knew, Alexandra was in my arms, and her body was warm and soft under my hands. I held her to me and felt her erect nipples rubbing across my breasts. Her breath was a soft and gentle caress. Her eyes stared deeply into mine.

She tried to pull herself away. "There's something crazy about this," she said. Dazed as I was, I noticed that her voice was a little slurred. "I can't figure it out." She giggled again. "Did someone put something in the drinks?"

"There haven't been any drinks." Now I started giggling. I felt totally stoned.

"Seriously, Chris," she said, trying to suppress her idiotic laughter. "Seriously. We have to keep our minds clear. We must." But then she started giggling again, and somehow we both slumped down together on the soft cushions. My hand fell carelessly upon her breast. Instinctively I caressed the full, soft shape of her flesh through the skimpy leotard. Then I eased the garment off her shoulder and rolled it down, revealing her pure pale skin. I pressed my cheek against her, letting my hair tumble down upon her. I kissed her breast and then gently took her nipple between my lips, licking and nibbling at it. I felt her hands circle around behind my head, pressing me harder against her. I heard her gasp and sigh.

I squirmed around, moving down to kiss the insides of her thighs. She seemed so beautiful, so sexy, I wanted to kiss her all over. I nipped the sensitive skin ever so gently with my teeth, then traced little lines up her flesh with the tips of my fingernails. Alexandra's hands clenched upon my shoulders. She let out a long moan.

I pulled her leotard all the way off. Then, feeling much too warm all of a sudden, I took off my own garment, too. And then I opened her legs and lowered my head toward her pink, wet cunt. I soon licked it delicately, relishing the taste of her as I tickled her clitoris with the tip of my tongue. Then I closed my lips over her cunt and pushed my tongue in deep, loving the way she trembled and gasped in response.

Men have always been my primary passion, but under the influence of the gas they'd piped into the basement, I felt so horny and so sensual that Alexandra looked like the most irresistible creature on earth. It was a delight to lick deep into her vagina. It was ecstasy to hear her cry out as she came.

At the same time, I was getting more and more turned on myself. And then I felt someone approach me from behind, as two warm, capable hands caressed my thighs. I flinched in surprise, but was overwhelmed at the same time by little trembling sensations that ran up my body and created a delicious aching need in my cunt.

I felt the legs of the person behind me pushing between my own legs. I felt his body hairs, his skin against my own. And when his fingers began to probe my wet pussy, it took my strength away. I soon forgot about my tender attentions toward Alexandra, and slid off her and lay facedown on the cushions, my face turned to one side, my eyes closed, as I savored the sensations of pure pleasure that the unknown man behind me was creating with his fingers.

Then I felt him move the head of his cock against my ass as he searched for the opening between my labes. I felt the heat of his body. I heard his breathing. I was totally open to him, totally defenseless. I wanted him inside me, filling me up.

He thrust deep. His cock was so large and so long that when he pushed in all the way it hurt just a tiny bit. But the pain was as sweet as the pleasure, and I wanted it, wanted it all. I heard him grunt with passion and I felt his hands reaching under me and grabbing hold of my breasts. He held them firmly, squeezing the soft flesh. He started fucking me hard, from behind. I no longer knew where I was, but heard myself moaning, writhing on the cushions, shamelessly pressing my hips against his groin, eager to hold every inch of him inside me.

Suddenly I came. It was an incredibly powerful orgasm, making me scream and whimper and claw at the soft pillows on which I lay.

He paused for a moment while my head cleared slightly. It suddenly seemed important to see my mystery lover. I squirmed around and turned half onto my side, without letting his cock come out of me. The room lights had been dimmed to the point where everything was dark and shadowy. I blinked for a moment and saw that a full-scale orgy had begun. Everyone was paired off, copulating in the semidarkness.

I reached for my lover. I wanted him beside me. I wanted to hold him and taste his kisses. As I looked up at him I saw that he was very muscular, a massive silhouette above me. His face was in shadow.

As if he sensed my needs, he shifted so that we were lying side by side, his cock still embedded in me. He took my face between his hands and kissed me very hard, thrusting his tongue between my lips. I loved it, every moment of it. I craved to be taken by him in every possible way.

He began fucking me again, and when he ground his hips against mine the pressure on my clitoris brought me almost instantly to orgasm for a second time. I clutched at him blindly and screamed with fulfillment. I wrapped my legs around him and held him deep, deep inside me. I ran my fingers across his face and down over his chest.

Again, just for a moment, my head cleared slightly, as if the orgasm temporarily freed me from the effects of the aphrodisiac gas. I looked at my lover and saw his face for the first time.

I cried out. This time it wasn't a cry of passion, but a cry of shock and dismay. "Josef!" I exclaimed. "Oh, God."

I started trying to pull free from him. The whole thing was now obvious. Dose the prisoners with an aphrodisiac until they become insatiable, then creep in and have sex with them. It was despicable. I shuddered at the thought that Carl and Helen Stanowski were probably in here with us as well, and that one of them could easily be the next to assault me.

"Let go," I gasped, trying to fight free of Josef's hands. But I felt dizzy and clumsy. My movements were uncoordinated. There was no strength in my muscles.

I heard him laugh. "Surely you're not satisfied already, Christina?" And he moved his hips, thrusting his cock deep into me again.

I gasped at the flood of sensations. He was right—I was so incurably horny I couldn't think straight.

"Wouldn't you like a little more?" he whispered to me in his deep voice, watching me, mocking me. Then he fucked me harder, and I cried out in despair as the sensations overwhelmed me.

He reached down and fingered my clitoris. "Why fight it when it feels so good?" he murmured to me. "Why not enjoy it? Why not, Christina?"

Already I was getting close to orgasm again. I knew I couldn't resist. And, to be totally, shamefully truthful, I knew that it wasn't only the effects of the aphrodisiac. I realized I felt a terrible ambivalent attraction toward this man. His incredible good looks and his aura of pure power turned me on, while at the same time I hated him for using and abusing me.

So I lay back and let him take me, giving myself up to the pure physical pleasure of his long, heavy cock invading my cunt, taking me in hard, angry strokes, his hands on my breasts squeezing almost painfully, his mouth upon mine. I gave myself up to it all.

This time, however, he didn't let me reach orgasm. Whenever he felt my body become tense and he heard my breathing quicken, he paused, making tantalizing little movements with his cock, holding me just short of coming. And then he took his cock out of me altogether.

I felt desperately empty and deprived. I reached for him.

One of his hands held me between the legs. His fingers lightly stroked between my labes and over my clitoris. "You still want more, Christina?"

"You know I do," I said, but hated him for making me say it. Unfortunately, I knew that he knew I wanted him. There was no point in pretending.

"Please me, and I will please you," he said, his lips

very close to my ear. I felt the warm touch of his breath.

I realized what he meant, and hesitated. But his fingers were still working insistently on my clitoris, and the aching need for fulfillment was a force much bigger than the force of rationality.

He sat up, continuing to touch me with one hand, and holding me against him with the other. My cheek pressed against his chest, and I could hear the pounding of his heart and feel the perspiration on his skin.

"Please me, and I will please you," he repeated.

I moved my head lower, then closed my eyes as I felt the tip of his cock against my lips. I opened my mouth wide and took him in deep, till his penis nudged the back of my throat. I began sucking, massaging the underside of his cock with my tongue, moving my head up and down. The last vestiges of my resistance had crumbled. All I could think of was the feel of his body against mine, the taste of his cock in my mouth, the sensations he was still producing with his fingers on my clitoris. It overwhelmed me. I wanted it all.

I started sucking him more and more greedily, feeling his rigid cock grow larger as his excitement became greater. The act that I had originally wanted to avoid became the act that I did not want to end. Once more I needed to have him in every possible way.

"I wanted you as soon as I saw you," I heard him saying, though I could hardly understand the words, I was so high on the aphrodisiac. "I wanted you. I wanted this." Then, gently, he pulled my head up so that his cock came out of my mouth. He stared at my face. "You see, Christina? I told you you would end up *wanting* to please me."

Before I could respond or reply, he pushed me over on my back and lay on top of me, holding me down with his arms. He pressed his legs between mine, opening my thighs, and guided his cock up and into me. At first I wanted to struggle and free myself from him, then I wanted him to thrust deeper into me. The two conflicting desires kept alternating, while the waves of sexual pleasure grew stronger and stronger, and I realized I no longer knew the difference between my own desires and the passion that the drug had instilled in me.

So I lay there as though I were helpless. He brought me to a shattering climax again, and then I felt my consciousness drifting away, as the sounds around me seemed distant. I vaguely sensed him getting up and leaving me, but I was in a half-world where everything was as vague and formless as a dream.

Gradually, very gradually, I passed out.

CHAPTER SIX

Although I woke up feeling groggy, eventually all my senses came back to me. The dreamlike eroticism of the previous evening was gone. The world suddenly seemed painfully real.

But I couldn't figure out where I was. I was still naked, lying across a pile of soft pillows. But were these the pillows on which I had had sex with Josef in the basement? No—because the floor was moving under me. I was in some kind of vehicle.

I sat up and managed to focus my eyes. My six fellow prisoners were lying all around me, all of them still unconscious. We were in the back of some kind of truck. It was windowless. The only illumination was from a small light in the center of the roof. The vehicle swayed and lurched from side to side, as if we were traveling over a rough back road.

My head hurt. My whole body, too, felt sore. I hugged my knees up to my breasts and winced at the ache that spread out from protesting muscles in my back. My hips felt stiff. And when I touched my most tender place, I found that my vagina was red and inflamed.

There had to be a way out of this nightmare. At least, that's what I told myself, wanting to believe that there was some hope for us all. I couldn't imagine where we were being taken next, and I didn't want to think about it. I didn't want to look forward to more evenings of drugged sex and humiliation. And I didn't want to have to deal with my strange ambivalence toward Josef. He was evil and irrational, probably insane, and if at the same time I found him sexually attractive, that attraction indicated an unhealthy aspect of myself that frightened me.

I stood up, steadying myself against the wall of the vehicle. I stepped over my fellow travelers and felt around the rear wall, where I assumed some doors might be. The surface seemed solid and unbroken, though in the dim light it was hard to tell. Some kind of Formica finish. I moved on around the space, feeling for a handle, an edge, anything. But all I found was a cubicle containing a small chemical toilet.

I gave up and sat down again. I saw Mark, the tall, lanky musician, roll over muttering to himself.

I realized I badly needed someone to talk to. I reached out and shook his shoulder. Within a couple of minutes he was awake. He sat up, and I could tell he was as disoriented as I had been when I first woke up.

I explained to him all I had discovered—that we were in a bus or a truck, and there seemed to be no way out. He seemed to take this philosophically. He just shrugged and grimaced. "I wish I had your easygoing outlook," I told him.

He shrugged again. "I try to go with the flow. Know what I mean?" he said. "Anyhow, I figure this can't last forever. And when we get loose, this is going to be great publicity." He grinned at me.

I laughed despite myself. It was too ridiculous. "I can do without publicity," I said.

"I can't. Know what I mean?" He coughed and winced. Evidently he had some sore muscles too. "That was some kind of weird scene last night," he said.

"I thought rock musicians get that kind of action all the time," I replied.

"Yeah. On tour sometimes. I'll tell ya, whatever that gas was, I'd like to buy some of it. Take a hit now and then. Whew. Beats amyls." He lay back down on the cushions on the floor. "What was your name again?" he asked me.

"Christina."

"Yeah. That's right. I'm Mark."

"I know."

"Yeah. Well, take it easy, Christina." He shut his eyes.

"You're not going to go to sleep again, are you?"

"Ain't nothing better to do," he observed. He rolled over, making himself more comfortable.

I swore silently to myself. I'd known musicians like Mark in the past—easygoing guys with a lot of charm, but completely useless if you had to depend on them for anything. Go with the flow, indeed. He'd go with the flow till it took him all the way downstream and over Niagara Falls.

Personally, I believed in going *against* the flow, to get whatever it was that I wanted. Especially in a situation like this.

I looked around, feeling someone moving behind me. It was Elizabeth, the actress, waking up. And Michel, beside her. So at least I was going to have some people to talk to.

"This is intolerable," Elizabeth said, as she realized where she was. "It is simply intolerable. Someone will have to do something. I can't take too much more of this. I simply can't."

She sounded so self-obsessed, as if she expected everyone to run around serving her. I couldn't help smiling.

"I don't know what you find amusing," she snapped

at me. "My God, we're in the hands of crazy people. Monsters." She peered around in the dimness. "Isn't there any kind of rest room in this thing?"

"Back there." I pointed to the little cubicle I had stumbled across.

"Does it have a mirror?"

I said no.

Elizabeth muttered something to herself. She stood up, trying to maintain as much dignity as possible under the circumstances, and made her way to the toilet, picking her way carefully around the cushions and the people lying upon them.

I turned to Michel. "Do you have any ideas?"

He smiled sadly and shrugged. "I find it very hard, accepting this that has happened to us," he said, with his slight Swiss accent softening the words. "There is a very important series of ski trials in Colorado this month. They have started already. I am too late now to go there and qualify."

My God, I thought to myself, he's still thinking about skiing. "Well, maybe next year," I said at random. "Assuming we get loose by then."

"Next year?" He shrugged. "Yes, but do you realize for such a short time, I am able to compete? I am getting old already, for this sport. And every day I am away from the slopes, I lose my reflexes, my skills."

"So we'd better figure how to get out of this mess as soon as we can, right?" I told him, as forcefully as I could.

He shrugged. "I do not see how." He seemed to have a kind of Germanic fatalism.

"Well, let's think about it, shall we?"

Again, the shrug of the shoulders.

We were silent for a while. The vehicle's engine note changed, and I had the impression we were picking up speed. The side-to-side lurching motion changed to a more gentle rhythm. I decided we had moved onto a freeway or interstate highway.

"I once trained as a swimmer," Michel said, after a few minutes. "I learned how to hold my breath for long periods. If I can remember those exercises, perhaps I could do them if we are given gas again. Yes?"

"Sure," I told him.

"But then what would I do?" he went on. "I am strong, but the one called Josef, he is strong too. Maybe more than me. A wrestler, I think. And there is still the problem of the drug." He gestured at his left arm, and the tiny mark where he, too, had been injected. "If we escape, how do we live?"

"There has to be an antidote," I told him.

"Perhaps. But could anyone find an antidote in the few hours we could stay alive?"

I sighed. "All right, all right, forget it. There's obviously no point in even thinking about how to get free." I stood up and moved away to the other end of the truck. His attitude of resignation was simply too depressing.

I sat hunched in the corner, hugging my arms across my breasts. I thought up a dozen different crazy plans and discarded them. I tried to close my eyes and let the rhythmic motion of the vehicle lull me. It didn't work too well.

After a while, Robert French regained consciousness, and then Alexandra, and Jane, the would-be starlet. I sat watching them unobtrusively as each of them realized in turn that we were no longer in the basement and were being transported somewhere.

French became typically enraged. He went around the space, pounding on the walls. He shouted a lot. Naturally, this didn't do any good.

Jane simply sat miserably on a cushion, staring blankly in front of her.

Alexandra managed to talk Robert out of his temper tantrum, then noticed me sitting quietly watching her. She came over and sat down beside me. "How are you feeling?" she asked me.

I looked at her face and remembered, very vividly, holding her and then making love to her under the influence of the aphrodisiac gas. "I guess I feel a little embarrassed," I told her.

"But it was nice, wasn't it?" she said, with a shy smile.

"Yes. Yes, that part was nice. What happened afterward wasn't so nice." I told her about Josef.

She shrugged. "At least you didn't have Carl Stanowski panting over you."

"You mean you did?"

"I think so. I can't even be sure, I was so high on that stuff. Chris, what the hell are we going to do?"

"That's what I asked our friends over there," I said, gesturing discreetly at our companions. "I didn't get too many answers."

"I know what you mean." Alexandra frowned. She moved closer to me, so that she could talk almost directly into my ear. "I figure with the noise of this bus, or whatever we're in, they can't easily bug our conversation," she murmured.

I nodded.

"The way I figure it," she went on, "is that if we're ever going to get loose from these crazies—I mean, the Stanowskis, and Josef—we'll have to take a supply of the drug with us, or else we won't be able to survive long enough for anyone to find how to make up a cure for it."

Once again I nodded.

"So I'm figuring on seducing Carl," she finished, quietly and matter-of-factly.

Judging from the look of revulsion on her face, the

idea didn't appeal to her. "You think you can go through with it?" I asked.

"I'll do whatever I have to. It won't be the first time I've had to take up with a man I didn't like. See, I haven't had an easy life, Chris. You inherited your money, right? I had to hustle to make mine. Anyway, what do you figure on doing?"

Her hazel eyes regarded me steadily. I realized that I already knew what I had to do. I just didn't want to admit it to myself. The prospect was too disturbing. "I guess I have to go for Josef," I said quietly. "See if I can seduce his fucked-up mind, as well as his body."

She nodded. "Good," she said. "I don't see any alternative, do you?"

I smiled grimly. "I could always try and make it with Helen Stanowski. "I'm damned sure she's got the hots for me."

"For you, for me, and for all the men, too," said Alexandra. "Why else do you think there are men in this group? To service that woman, that's why. No, she is altogether too weird. You wouldn't get anywhere with her. Although you can bet that all the guys here will end up giving it a try."

"You think so?"

"They're eventually going to get desperate. They'll try anything."

Her tone of voice frightened me as much as what she said. She sounded grim, and utterly convinced that she was speaking the truth.

CHAPTER SEVEN

The journey lasted several hours. I tried to sleep some more, since it seemed I was going to need all the rest I could get. Some of the others talked among themselves, going over the same ground again and again—where we were being taken, what we should do when we got there, and how Robert French would crucify our captors if he ever got them in a courtroom. None of the talk amounted to anything; I was convinced that Alexandra and I had the only workable plan.

I did finally drift off to sleep, then woke up suddenly when the truck moved off the main highway and started bumping over a back road, the tires kicking up gravel.

"It can't be much longer now," French said, in a suddenly decisive voice. He was standing at one end of the space, bracing himself as the vehicle lurched from side to side. "I've decided—the only way is to try and make a break when they open up the doors to transfer us into the place where they plan to keep us. That's the right moment. If we don't try to get loose then, we'll be stuck in another basement, or worse, and there'll be absolutely no hope after that."

He stared at the rest of us, challenging us to disagree with him. He seemed even more tense than before, breathing quickly, absentmindedly flexing his free hand.

Michel shook his head wearily. "We have not yet been given today's dose of the drug, the chemical that they have addicted us to," he said, his Swiss accent softening the words. "If you escape, you will last perhaps six hours." He shrugged.

"Defeatism," French snapped back. "All I know is, someone has to do something. And if the rest of you won't help me, I'll do it alone."

The truck slowed down, moving up what felt like a steep grade. And then it stopped completely. There was a long pause. Somewhere up front, a door slammed. We heard faint voices.

There was a scraping, rattling sound from the rear of the truck. A key turned. Then the rear doors swung open.

Brilliant sunlight came blazing through. All of us had lost track of the time; personally, I had figured it must be late evening. Our eyes had become accustomed to the very dim light inside the truck. The afternoon sun was so bright it hurt. No doubt our captors had planned it that way.

"Quickly, now." It was Josef's voice, from just outside the vehicle. "All of you. Get out." He sounded impatient and commanding.

Steps had been moved up against the rear of the truck. I stumbled down them with my fellow prisoners, still blinded by the sunlight. I winced as my bare feet stepped onto the hot gravel. We seemed to be in some kind of desert area. Jagged gray mountains shimmered through heat-haze. There was a big wooden building right in front of us, its door standing open, all its windows boarded up.

"Inside!" Josef commanded. I noticed he had a gun in his hand. "Get in there."

I didn't need to be told; my feet were burning. But Robert French had other ideas. He suddenly turned and ran.

I stopped and watched him sprint away around the

truck. He hesitated, then headed away down the dirt road which had brought us there.

Josef grabbed my arm. His grip made me wince. "Get inside," he snapped at me, and pushed me so hard that I half fell through the open door of the building, joining the others already in there.

I looked back to see if Josef would go after French, but he ignored the man, strode into the building after us, and slammed the door. "We will collect Mr. French in a little while," he said, with a faint, malicious smile. "After he has had time to enjoy the pleasures of drug withdrawal and desert sun." He sounded absolutely confident, and not at all surprised by what French had done. I felt my spirits sinking, faced with this implacable giant who seemed to have everything so much under his control. "Now," he went on, "you will get acquainted with your new home here. Down those steps." He gestured to a flight of stairs that seemed to offer the only way out of the claustrophobic, windowless room we had been pushed into. "And please remember," he added, hefting the automatic in his right hand, "I can protect myself."

Yes, I thought, descending the stairs—he could protect himself easily from any threat of physical violence. Maybe, though, he would be more vulnerable to seduction. I intended to take the first possible opportunity of finding out.

We were herded down a hallway in the basement of the building. The place had looked derelict from the outside, but down here it had been modernized, with clean white walls, bright lights, and carpeting.

There was a series of doors leading off the hallway. Josef directed one of us through each of the doors. No one liked the idea of being split off from the group, but he didn't give anyone much choice. When my turn came, he hustled me roughly through the doorway, ignoring my token protests, and then slammed the door behind me. I heard a key turn in the lock.

I found myself in a little room containing a bed and a bureau, but no other furniture. There was no window, of course, and the only light came from a bulb recessed behind a thick glass panel in the ceiling. I squinted up and saw what looked like a closed-circuit TV camera alongside the light. I was under surveillance.

I discovered a tiny bathroom adjoining my room. It contained a shower, a washbasin, a chemical toilet that seemed brand-new but smelled unpleasantly of disinfectant.

I went back into the bedroom. It was oddly quiet, I realized. "Alexandra!" I shouted, remembering she'd been put in the room beside mine. But when I stopped and listened, I couldn't hear a thing. The walls must have been made of concrete. And when I inspected the door I saw it was made of steel and shut very tightly. Obviously Josef was security-minded, and he didn't want us to communicate with each other.

I sat down on the bed and tried to come to terms with the situation. On the negative side, there was no way around it: We were captive, maybe for a good long while, and Josef and the Stanowskis could do more or less anything they wanted with us.

On the positive side, it looked as if they didn't intend any physical harm. In fact, the place had been set up purely for pleasure—Josef's pleasure—though maybe if I tried to adopt the right attitude it wouldn't have to be painful for me, either. Maybe the trick was to resign myself to it, the way that Mark, the rock musician, had. After all, Josef wasn't bad-looking. In fact, I had to admit, he was incredibly handsome, and had charisma, too. Of course, he was power-mad . . . and then there was Carl Stanowski to think about . . . but he was

Alexandra's problem. The more I thought about Josef, the more I thought maybe I could get my hooks into him, and eventually win him over.

Suddenly, as if someone had been reading my mind, the door of my room opened and Josef walked in.

CHAPTER EIGHT

He shut the door carefully behind him and stood staring down at me a moment, toying with a bunch of keys. I stared back, tilting my chin up, trying to look more confident than I felt. Secretly I was thinking that I must look a wreck after all that had happened, with no makeup and not even a chance to brush my hair. On the other hand, I knew how he liked the look of my body in the leotard he had made me wear. So I arched my back a little, making my breasts push out toward him. I noticed him glance down at them, then back at my face.

"Sit on the bed," he said. His voice was quiet, barely a murmur, but there was no mistaking the commanding tone.

I paused as if I were thinking it over, and then I turned and walked to the bed and sat down, taking my time. Once again he looked at me, and I stared steadily back. I could see his broad chest rising and falling under the black silk shirt he was wearing. I noticed he was breathing slightly faster.

"What do you want?" I asked, keeping my voice carefully neutral.

He smiled as if I amused him slightly. "I have to get a little better acquainted with all of my guests," he said. "One by one."

"And I'm first on the list?" I folded my arms under

my breasts, cradling them so that they almost pushed out of the top of the leotard. "I'm flattered."

He frowned and moved toward me. He reached out and curled his fingers in my hair, closing his hand into a fist. He turned his wrist, making me tilt my head back. I winced as he tugged and tightened his grip. "Remember, my dear Christina," he said, still in the soft, low voice that now sounded oddly dangerous, "you are mine to play with as I wish. You should show an appropriate degree of respect." With the last word he gave a sudden jerk of his arm, pulling my hair hard. I cried out, but then he released his grip and put his hands on his hips. "You understand?" he said.

"Yes." I looked away from his dark eyes, realizing I had acted too fresh, too feisty. "I understand."

"I understand—master," he corrected me, still staring at me.

I thought the words would catch in my throat, but I managed to echo him. "I understand, master."

"Good." He sounded more relaxed, and I sensed the tension easing. He cupped my chin in his hand. His grip was firm and deliberate, and I realized he had rigid self-control. I didn't have to fear his being the kind of unbalanced guy liable to lose his cool and do something dangerously crazy. So long as I did what he wanted, there wouldn't be any trouble—I might even enjoy some of it. And sooner or later, I was sure I could get through to him.

He bent down. His black-bearded, tanned face moved close to mine. He held my jaw as if he thought I might pull away. I smelled some kind of after-shave he was wearing, and heard the slight sound of his breathing. His face came close, and still closer, and then his mouth pressed against mine.

At first I kept my eyes open. But so did he, and

seeing him staring at me bothered me. So I closed my eyes as my lips yielded to him.

I tried to seem willing as he kissed me. My mouth opened under his. I responded to him, moving my head and returning the force of the kiss.

He shifted his hands and held my head between his palms. The kiss lasted a long time, and I have to admit it turned me on a little. I told myself that it was just an aftereffect of the aphrodisiac gas we'd been given the previous night; but in fact Josef was a powerfully erotic man. It was a sensual kiss. I felt his sexuality, and I couldn't help responding to it.

Finally he released me and stood up. He was breathing heavily, and I noticed a bulge in the crotch of the tight pants he was wearing.

"Do I please you?" I asked him, thinking that was the kind of thing he wanted to hear.

He nodded slowly. "Stand up, now," he told me, and stepped back a pace.

I got to my feet and clasped my hands behind my back, acting the part of the obedient slave, which he seemed to want.

He walked around me, studying my body. Then he sat down on the bed. Casually he unzipped his fly and pulled out his cock. It was big and hard, and he massaged one finger over a bead of moisture at the tip. "Walk up and down," he told me, his eyes watching me carefully.

There wasn't much space in the tiny bedroom, and I wasn't exactly sure what he wanted. I took a couple of steps toward the little bathroom, then a couple of steps back.

"Pull your shoulders back more," he told me. "Push your breasts out. Yes. And don't look in my direction. Look straight ahead. That's right. That's good."

Out of the corner of my eye I saw him rubbing the

underside of his cock, smiling faintly to himself. I kept walking up and down, displaying myself for him while he devoured me with his eyes. It wasn't an unpleasant feeling, either; I always enjoy showing myself off to an appreciative audience. He made me feel very desirable, and it aroused me, just as it aroused him.

"All right," he said, after a moment more, "come and kneel in front of me. Here." And he pointed at the floor by his feet.

I'd been expecting that. I guess I should have resented being ordered around like a servant, but I'd made up my mind to seduce this man and make myself so erotic for him that in the end he'd be addicted to me—he would, in fact, become my slave, rather than vice versa. So any way I could please him was an advantage from my point of view. It would help me achieve my goal more quickly.

I knelt before him without a murmur. I let my arms lie passively at my sides and looked up at him as if waiting for instructions.

"You know what I want," he said, his eyes half closed, his cock standing up very heavy and rigid in his grip.

I looked down demurely. I licked my lips, then bent forward and took him into my mouth. I closed my eyes and started sucking him, moving my head gently.

He was impatient. I felt his hands in my hair, suddenly tugging, pulling my head down. "Deeper," he told me. His voice was sharp and louder than before. "Much deeper . . . ah!"

He relaxed his grip as I obeyed him and accepted the whole length of his cock, opening my throat to him. He was very large, and for a moment I almost gagged. Then I shifted position slightly and started rocking my head up and down in a steady rhythm, caressing the underside of his cock with my tongue.

He groped down and took hold of my breasts through the thin material of the leotard. His fingers clenched them, gently at first, then hard, making me wince. But he wasn't so rough as to cause real pain, and the power of this man was actually continuing to arouse me.

Anytime I find someone at all attractive I can usually get off on giving him oral sex, and Josef was no exception. His cock, so big and hot in my mouth, felt as if it would feel even better in my pussy.

He pinched my nipples with his fingers and thumbs. He moved his hips, thrust his cock deep in my mouth, then withdrew it. He grunted with pleasure.

"Now sit on me," he told me in a low voice.

I stood up, wiping my mouth on the back of my hand. It took me a moment to catch my breath. I reached between my legs for the fastening of the leotard. "You want me to take this off?"

"Just undo it down there. Then kneel on the bed. One knee on each side, straddling my hips."

I did as he told me.

"Now sit down." I felt him move the head of his cock between my labes.

"I'm not very wet," I said uneasily, afraid that his cock might hurt me.

"Sit down," he repeated. He took me by the shoulders and pulled me onto him.

I realized that if he hurt me a little, forcing his way in, that would just demonstrate his mastery over me. So I did as he commanded, and his cock inched into me as I lowered my hips. Actually I was wetter than I'd realized, and it hardly hurt at all. But I made a show of wincing and even whimpering a little as he slid inside. I closed my eyes and bit my lip, frowning and clenching my fists. Then, when the whole length of him was embedded in me, I let out a moan.

He grunted and moved his hips, wriggling them to

and fro. I felt his hands at my breasts again. This time he took hold of the leotard and jerked it down, ripping the fabric. Then his fingernails raked my skin.

"Up and down, Christina," he murmured to me. "Fuck yourself on me. Do it." His voice was a little strained. He was very, very turned on.

I started moving, slowly at first, then faster. Within a minute I was bouncing up and down on him, bracing myself with my hands on his shoulders. I heard his breathing become hoarse. His hands clutched my tits, then moved behind me and grabbed my ass. His whole body stiffened before he came, gasping and wrenching his hips up so that he held himself jammed up into me.

His breathing slowed, and he let go of me. He sighed. "Very nice," he murmured. "Very, very nice. Get up, now."

Obediently I swung one leg over him and pulled free. His cock came out of me, semierect and wet with my juices and his own semen. I felt halfway aroused myself— not aching for an orgasm, but definitely in the mood. Still, that was obviously of no interest to him. In his plan I was merely a servant to be used for his pleasure. Little did he realize I had a plan of my own.

Josef stood up, put his penis away inside his pants, and zipped his fly. He was much more relaxed than when he had first come into the room, and he grinned at me. "I can see you're going to be a very good member of our group, Christina," he said. "I'm so glad that you got rid of the defiant attitude that you displayed yesterday. It wasn't going to do you any good. Things will be much easier, and much more enjoyable, this way."

I nodded demurely.

"The more you please me, the more favors I can do for you," he added, reaching out and stroking my hair. "We can improve this bare little room. I can get clothes for you. And perhaps you would like some other things—a hairbrush, toothbrush, maybe even a larger room altogether." He bent his head to mine and kissed me. His tongue pushed into my mouth. I could feel that, despite just having come, he was still full of passion. "You understand?" he murmured.

"I understand—master."

He pulled back and laughed. "Very good," he said, patting my cheek. "Christina, I can see you will be a very special erotic partner." He reached down and rubbed his fingers across one of my nipples. "Very special, and most beautiful." He studied me, savoring the look of me.

"May I—" I hesitated as if I was afraid to speak up. "May I ask you a question?"

He paused as if deciding whether to allow it. Then he nodded. His eyes suddenly became more watchful—he would be quick to catch any sign of insincerity or rebellion on my part.

"I just want to know how long we'll be here," I blurted out, "and what's going to happen—"

He held up his hand. "You have already been told: This is a self-contained community. It will last indefinitely, for as long as I choose. And we exist to please each other, Christina. All of us."

There was something weird about the way he said this. The words came out mechanically, as if they were a speech he'd learned and repeated many times. It wasn't at all the way he'd been talking a moment earlier. I began to wonder if Josef had more secrets than I had guessed. I wondered, in fact, if what he was saying was entirely true.

I didn't have time to ask. He buttoned his shirt brusquely. "You will wash and put on a clean leotard—they're in one of the drawers of that chest," he told me. "You will be ready for a meeting of the group in one hour from now.'' He reached for the door, then hesitated, as if there were something else he wanted to say, something a little more personal, perhaps.

But he thought better of it. He opened the door quickly, strode out, and locked it behind him.

CHAPTER NINE

I washed, put on the clean leotard, and then waited.

More than once I instinctively looked at my left wrist, only to remember again that they had taken my wristwatch when they took all my other personal property.

The white walls of the little room seemed to close in on me, and the total silence of the place got on my nerves. I wondered how people in prisons managed to endure solitary confinement. I was accustomed to an active life that was completely under my control; being trapped with absolutely nothing to do was almost unbearable.

Then I realized that they probably hoped it would bother me. It was part of their plan. But realizing this made the whole situation easier for me to deal with. I'm good at meeting challenges.

I lay down on the bed, closed my eyes, and chose something to keep my mind occupied: mental arithmetic. I started with number 1, doubled it to make 2, doubled it to make 4 . . . and so on. Since I'm not very good at math, I kept losing track and having to start again. That was OK, however—the longer it took, the better.

When I eventually heard a key turn in the lock of my door, I'd reached 262,144. And I was pretty sure I was feeling a lot more together and alert than they intended me to be.

I looked up as the door opened. It was Helen Stanowski.

"Christina," she said, stony-faced. "You will come at once."

"Yeah?" I grinned cheerfully. "I bet you say that to all the girls." And then, before she could reply, I jumped up off the bed and stepped quickly into the corridor.

She caught my arm. Her grip was deliberately painful, digging in just above the elbow. "I will not tolerate insults," she said.

"Really, it was only a joke." I looked at her coolly.

She stared back at me, then seemed to decide that the conversation wasn't worth the effort. She let go of my arm and walked ahead, along the hallway to a door at the end. "This is the communal meeting room," she said, opening the door. "You will wait in it."

"All right," I agreed, "I will." I had decided it was advisable to antagonize Helen Stanowski. That way, she'd be less likely to want sex with me in any of the group scenes which I was sure would be happening in the days ahead. Also, if she disliked me while Josef became infatuated with me, I could generate conflict between the two of them.

I walked past Helen, into the room. She slammed the door behind me.

I looked around. It was like the last basement we'd been kept in—where we'd had the orgy. Wall-to-wall carpet, pillows to sit on, and not much else.

Mark, Michel, and Alexandra were already in there. Alexandra ran over and gave me a hug. "Good to see you," she said. "I tried banging on the wall, I tried shouting, but I guess the rooms where they put us were soundproofed."

"Yes," I agreed. "They don't want us to communicate.'' I nodded hello to the two men, then sat down with Alexandra.

"I've been so fucking bored I'm nearly out of my mind,'' she told me. Her words tumbled out quickly. She took hold of my hand. "I can't stand being alone.''

"That's the way they want you to feel,'' I said. "Try not to let it get to you.'' I lowered my voice. "Say— did you have any visitors?''

She frowned. "No. No, I've been stuck on my own ever since they brought us down here. You?''

I nodded. "Josef,'' I said. "And I think he may be easier to influence than we thought.'' My voice was a barely audible whisper; I was sure that, even if they had the room bugged, no one would be able to hear what I was saying.

"That's great, Chris.'' Alexandra squeezed my arm. "I—'' She broke off, as the door into the room opened and Helen Stanowski appeared with Elizabeth, the aging glamour queen.

"Wait in here,'' said Helen. She slammed the door before Elizabeth could argue.

"They're bringing us in one by one?'' I asked Alexandra.

She nodded. "Safer for them that way, I guess.''

So we waited while the others were brought in one at a time. Everyone was complaining about being locked up for a couple of hours with nothing to do. Even Mark, the musician, seemed on edge. I decided to keep it a secret between Alexandra and myself that Josef had paid me a special visit.

Finally, we were all there except for Robert French. And then the door opened one last time, and Helen Stanowski came in with her brother, Carl, followed by the tall, broad-shouldered figure of Josef, all dressed in black. Then, right behind him, was French.

I winced when I saw the state he was in. His skin

was sunburned bright red. His face was slick with sweat, and he was breathing through swollen, cracked lips. His legs were covered in scratches, as if he'd been wading through brambles. His hands were handcuffed behind his back, and he was wearing a leather collar with a leash attached. Josef led him into the room like a dog, then pushed him down on the floor, turned, and walked to the center of the room.

I scrambled over to French and touched his shoulder. "Robert? Robert, are you all right?"

He didn't answer. There was a strange, blank look in his eyes.

"Mr. French has been given a mild tranquilizer," Josef said, his voice booming loud in the silence of the room. "He has me to thank for saving his life. The temperature outside is over 120 degrees every afternoon. If you're stupid enough to walk around half naked in the open sun, the heat can kill you within just a few hours. I found Mr. French stumbling around in circles."

He waited. There was a long silence.

"I think you should get Robert some water," said Michel.

"He has already had a little water. More, at this point, would not be good. I realize you don't like to see your companion suffer, but frankly I think Robert French deserves to suffer a little. It will undoubtedly make him more cooperative in the future." He smiled coldly and rubbed his hands slowly together.

Watching Josef, I couldn't decide how much of his sadism was an act. He'd been a lot easier to deal with when he'd been alone with me in my room. There he was still a dictator, for sure; but he hadn't seemed so threatening.

"Well." He put his hands on his hips. "Enough of Mr. French. I welcome you all to this place, where we will build our new community together. As you see, we have already taken a lot of trouble to modernize the building. We have installed air conditioning throughout, and all the basic comforts are provided. And—in case you are wondering—security is very, very tight. Just now, I went with my friends Helen and Carl and reset the combination lock on the one and only exit, upstairs on the ground floor. The combination is a six-digit number, and Helen, Carl, and myself know only two digits each. Therefore, it is impossible for anyone to leave unless all three of us cooperate in working the lock." He paused to let this sink in. I got the message: Even if a couple of us somehow jumped, say, Helen Stanowski, and tried to force her to release us, she knew only two digits of the lock combination.

"The exit door is steel-reinforced, set into a four-inch-thick steel frame," Josef went on. "This building, which was once a primitive warehouse for storing bauxite, is built of thick wood planks cemented together, and all the windows upstairs are boarded up and covered with concrete. So you see, even if you were able to get out of the basement, you would have no chance of escape. We are all in this together, my friends," he said chuckling wickedly. "Together, for as long as I choose."

"Just tell me one thing, mister." It was Elizabeth's voice. She stood up. "Tell me why, that's all. I mean what the hell is the point?" She gestured wildly. "If you want money—"

Josef walked over to her. He stopped just a couple of inches away and stood staring at her, just short of actually touching her.

She took a step back. I could see that, behind her bluster, she was scared of him.

"Sit down, Elizabeth," he said, very softly.

"But I just want to know—" Her voice was no longer strident. It was a whine.

"I said, sit down." He pointed at the floor. "You will learn to obey me, Elizabeth."

She glanced at the floor, then back at him. "I—"

He slapped her cheek. He moved incredibly quickly; the blow surprised me as much as it did her. The smack sounded very loud. Everyone stared.

Elizabeth clutched her cheek wordlessly.

Josef once again pointed at the floor.

This time, Elizabeth sank slowly down, first on one knee, and then backward onto a cushion.

"Good," said Josef. "Now that you have obeyed me, I will answer your question." He was as cool and controlled as ever. The incident hadn't ruffled him even slightly. "As I have already told each of you," he went on, "money is not relevant here. This is an experiment in communal living. Free from the interference of a moralistic, prudish outside world. We will live according to a code that I have written. We will enjoy an ideal society: beautiful women and handsome men, everyone healthy, successful, and desirable. We will please each other. In particular, you will all endeavor to please me." He spread his hands. "Self-centered, I admit; but who wouldn't be, if he had the power? And so long as you are all cooperative, it will be quite pleasant. Remember, all your needs will be catered to."

"All *my* needs?" Mark spoke up. "You got a guitar here, man?" He was lying stretched out with his hands behind his head, propped on a pillow. He was acting as cool and casual as ever, but I thought I detected some tension in him that hadn't been there before.

"A guitar? You wish to keep in practice?" Josef said condescendingly, as if trying to humor a child.

"I need music. Music's my life, man. Without music—" Mark shrugged. "I could go crazy in here."

Josef nodded. "I am sure each of you has certain special needs. No doubt some of you feel the pressure of time, and would like wristwatches. Some of you will dislike being unable to brush your teeth; others will be cold at night and will want extra blankets.'' He stared at us one by one, and I think he savored the knowledge that he was right—that we would, indeed, crave these small creature comforts. ''Well,'' he went on, ''I can supply the items you want. But you will have to earn them. By doing chores here, and by displaying good conduct. These sheets,'' he said, walking over to Carl Stanowski, who handed him some pages, ''outline the duties you will be expected to perform, and the points awarded for them. You will also see the points that will be deducted for each act of disobedience or misconduct.'' Again, the nasty smile. ''You see, you'll earn points and trade them in for what you want, just like green stamps. Five points will earn you a toothbrush; or in your case, Mark, perhaps a thousand points will earn you your musical instrument.''

''Christ, man!'' Mark slowly started getting up onto his feet. ''What is this shit? Is this a joke or something?'' He stared at Josef as if he couldn't believe the man was for real. ''I tell you, I'm serious. I get kind of crazy if I don't have music.''

''I, too, am serious.'' Josef said, handing Mark one of the printed sheets. ''Just how serious, you may not believe right now. But you soon will.''

Mark frowned, peering at the paper in his hand. He ran his fingers through his long, shaggy hair. ''I don't know, man,'' he muttered. ''I don't know.'' He sank back down on the floor, reading the document.

Josef walked around the room, distributing one page to each of us. ''You will have ample time to read and absorb the details later,'' he said. ''Now, it is time for you to take your medication, and then to eat, and then—then, to enjoy ourselves. Oh, by the way, if any of you have wondered about it, the supply of the medication is kept in a safe upstairs. And, as in the case of the exit door, the combination of the safe is shared among the three of us. We wouldn't want you to have more than one day's supply of the drug at a time. It might encourage you to feel independent. And, my friends, I can't emphasize this enough: Independence is something you no longer have. You depend totally on us. Without us—'' He shrugged. ''Without us, you die.''

CHAPTER TEN

So there we were: trapped in the basement, and even if we managed to find a way up to the ground floor we'd still be locked in; if we somehow broke out we wouldn't survive more than a few hours in the desert heat; and if we beat the heat we'd die from being deprived of the drug we were hooked on.

I could see the others trying to adjust to the feeling of total helplessness that Josef had created. As for me, I knew more certainly than ever that I had to get the better of him. If I could get *him* erotically addicted to me, everything else would fall into place. Otherwise . . .

He came around with a tray of paper cups of water, and gave one cup and one white pill to each of us. I gave him a shy smile when he came over to me. Then I bit my lip and stared at the floor as if I were too shy to look him in the eye.

He reached out casually and squeezed my shoulder, just for a moment. But it was enough.

He turned to address the group again. "I am giving you your medication late this evening," he said. "I wanted you to feel the beginnings of drug withdrawal. Some of you are a bit light-headed, right? Breathing faster than usual? Feeling slightly faint?" He grinned and nodded as he saw each of us realizing that, sure enough, we felt the way he described. "You see," he went on, "the drug does do what I said it will do.

I strongly advise you, never miss your daily dose.''

He walked to a door opposite where we had entered the room. He unlocked the door and opened it. ''In here are kitchen facilities, similar to those where you were my guests before. Help yourselves to the food in the refrigerator. Eat well; you're going to need your strength.''

He walked back to the Stanowskis. He moved with a swagger, conscious of how he had intimidated everyone. They were staring at him now like scared children. Even Alexandra looked meek and fearful.

''Take Mr. French to his room,'' Josef told Carl. ''And I will see you both later.''

With that, he walked out. Helen and Carl went over to French, lifted him under the arms, and took him away with them. They locked the exit after them.

''Well,'' I said loudly, determined to break the somber mood that had settled over everyone, ''Let's eat. I mean, there's nothing any of us can do. So how about it?'' I gestured toward the kitchen.

Alexandra managed a weak smile, and went to check out the refrigerator. Michel walked over to me. ''You have looked at this document?'' he said, holding up the list of rules we'd been given.

''Not yet.'' I gestured to where I'd folded it and tucked it in the neck of my leotard.

He nodded slowly. ''Read it, Christina. It is like being a child in a school, where the head teacher is a madman, and the children are never allowed to go home.''

With that, he went past me into the kitchen.

I sighed, took out the sheet, unfolded it, and scanned it. First was a list of incredibly detailed, petty tasks, each one worth some points of credit. Cleaning your room got you two points. Snitching on your friends—reporting remarks disloyal to the commune—got you ten points. Keeping a diary, for some reason, was worth one point per daily entry. At the other end of the scale, giving special sexual pleasure to Josef was worth twenty.

Next on the page were listed misdemeanors and penalties. For unresponsiveness: minus two points. For refusing to obey a command the first time: minus ten points. The same command a second time: solitary confinement for twenty-four hours, and minus twenty points. And so it went.

Lastly, there was a list of goodies, from toothbrushes to bed pillows, worth a certain number of points each.

I almost laughed. It was so blatant: the carrot and the stick. Too blatant to work, surely; who would take this seriously?

Then I thought ahead, and realized how seriously we had to take this sheet if we wanted any basic comforts at all. Josef's game was childish and degrading, but we had no choice. It was, after all, the only game in town—and it was his town. Already I found myself wondering whether my little love scene with him had earned me twenty points . . . and whether my insolence to Helen Stanowski had cost me ten.

We spent the next half hour eating cold food from the refrigerator. There was wine to drink, too—a couple of gallons of it. Everyone had one or two paper cups full, but Mark downed six or seven. We needed it to neutralize the tension of our situation.

Josef had known we'd all get a little drunk. That, too, was part of his plan. About an hour later, when the wine had had time to take effect, he came back into the communal basement room.

As soon as he appeared, all conversation stopped. He stood there a moment and surveyed the scene. He knew we didn't know what to expect from him, and he obviously liked to keep us guessing for as long as possible.

He walked slowly around the room, eyeing each of

us in turn. One wall was partially covered by drapes; he reached behind them and pulled a cord. The drapes drew aside, revealing a floor-to-ceiling mirror. At the same time, the lights dimmed.

A more intimate setting for our pleasures,'' he said in his deep, resonant voice. ''And now we can admire our own images.''

He strolled back into the center of the room. He had changed into a full-length black silk robe covered with stylized erotic art embroidered in gold and silver thread. The robe covered him from his neck to his bare feet, but I had no doubt that he was naked under it.

He stood and studied us again. Then he walked deliberately over to Jane, the busty blonde.

He reached out casually and took hold of one of her breasts. She instinctively flinched away.

Quickly—he had the trained reflexes of a fighter—he reached out with his other hand and grabbed her by her hair. I remembered when he had held me that way, and how it had half angered me, half excited me to feel the power of the man.

''There is really no point in resisting,'' he said softly, winding her hair around his fist, and digging his other hand down between her wide, heavy breasts.

I wondered why he hadn't got us horny with the aphrodisiac gas that we'd been given the previous night. Maybe he thought the wine would be enough. Or, more likely, he figured that a drugged audience was no fun. It was conquering us that turned him on. Ideally, I realized, he wanted to crush our resistance so thoroughly that we'd do anything—absolutely anything—he said, without question. He was like an animal trainer. Was that how he saw us? As circus animals?

He bent and brought his face close to Jane's. She swallowed hard. Her eyes were nervous. She raised her hands and pressed them against his chest, as if to hold him away from her. But it was a token struggle. He pulled her head up, still holding her by the hair. Ignoring her nervousness, he continued to be a little rough. He then forced his mouth hard against hers, and at the same time let go of her breasts and curled his arm behind her waist, dragging her to him.

We all watched, not knowing what else to do. He kissed her long and hard, and for a while she seemed to be responding. But then she seemed to have second thoughts and started to struggle. She pushed at him, harder; and then she reached up, grabbed at his face, and tried to rake him with her nails.

I experienced a sinking feeling in my stomach. I knew there was going to be trouble.

Josef let go of her at once. She backed away from him, wiping her mouth. Her hair was tousled and her leotard was pulled down, completely revealing her left breast. She tugged at the garment, trying to cover herself.

Josef stood for a moment, studying her. His expression was unreadable—totally controlled.

"Come here," he said slowly, deliberately.

She didn't say anything. She took another step back.

"I will count to three," he told her. "If, after I count three, you do not come here, I will punish you."

The sinking feeling in my stomach got worse. I wished Jane had the sense not to make a big deal out of this. Damn it, we'd all had sex together last night; what difference did it make? I was sure, too, she'd made it at various times in her life with a whole lot of men less attractive than Josef. But something about the situation was freaking her out.

"One," Josef counted. "Two." He watched her, and paused before the final count.

"No," Jane said in a pathetic voice.

"Three," said Josef. He didn't wait a moment longer. He moved forward in a swirl of his robe, amazingly

fast for such a large man. I half expected Mark or
Michel to try and defend Jane, but neither of them did.

She put up her hands to ward him off, but he caught
her wrists, pulled them behind her, then turned her and
forced her arms up. She cried out with a pathetic,
whimpering noise and had to stoop forward as he pushed
her wrists higher behind her back.

"Kneel," he told her, still in his controlled, impas-
sive voice. He tightened his hold on her.

She fell down onto her knees. Josef kicked a cushion
in front of her. "Lie across the cushion," he told her,
forcing her down onto it.

She subsided under him with another little moan. He
kept hold of her wrists with one of his big hands,
pinning her facedown across the cushion with her ass in
the air. He slid his free hand under her leotard between
her thighs and undid it, completely baring the cheeks of
her ass. Then he started spanking her.

His wide, heavy hand came down in hard, deliberate
strokes. She twisted and whimpered and tried to pull
free, but he had her easily pinned. The smacking of his
hand on her ass never once changed its rhythm. I saw
the white skin bounce and quiver under the blows. It
quickly turned bright red. Her whimpers grew louder
and became cries of distress. I knew that although the
spanking appeared harmless enough, and almost comic,
it probably hurt a lot more than it looked. Josef was a
powerful man, and I could see him bracing himself and
grunting with the effort of each blow. He went on, and
on; sweat beaded his forehead, and he began breathing
more heavily.

Jane began pleading with him. "I'm sorry!" she
blurted out. "I'm sorry, I didn't mean it! Oh please—
you're hurting me! Please stop! Oh, please will you
stop! Please!"

For a long time he ignored her cries and went on

mercilessly spanking her. Finally, he paused. "You are ready to please me now, Jane?" He asked her.

She swallowed hard and nodded helplessly.

Josef grabbed her bright red ass and dug his finger-nails into the tender skin. "You will speak to me. You will say, 'I will please you now.' "

She flinched in his grip. "I will please you!" she gasped.

"Good." But he kept hold of her, still letting her feel the edge of his nails. "I think, though, Jane, I need to hear more. I need to hear you tell me what you will do to please me, when I release my grip on you."

There was an uneasy pause. "I'll kiss you, and—" She broke off. "Oh, please, let me up. Please—"

He clenched his hand on her ass again. "You will please me, Jane, by sucking my cock. Am I correct?"

"Oh, please, let me go!"

"Am I correct?" he repeated, tightening his grip.

The last of the fight went out of her. "I—yes, I will—suck you," she blurted out.

"Good." He let go of her at last and stood up, glancing around at the rest of us. None of us could look him in the eye. I think we all felt guilty about not having tried to help Jane—but how could any of us make a stand, being so completely under Josef's con-trol? And why make a stand over this incident, anyway, since all he wanted from her was what she had undoubt-edly done the previous night?

Slowly, Jane got up onto her feet. Her face was flushed. She turned her head, avoiding looking at Josef.

He parted his robe. His cock was fully erect, standing out stiff and hard. He stroked his hand along the length of it. "Jane?" he said softly, dangerously.

She took a step closer, then got down on her knees. She licked her lips and reached up with her left hand.

He caught her wrist. "You will keep your hands behind your back," he told her.

She hesitated, then did as he told her.

He moved closer, taking hold of his own cock and guiding it to her mouth. Her lips parted. She closed her eyes and tilted her head back, and he started moving his hips in a steady rhythm, to and fro, gently pushing himself in and out of her mouth.

With each thrust, he probed a little deeper. I saw Jane gulping and realized she was gagging on the length of him. He was very big, and she obviously couldn't take it all the way. She tried, but ultimately she pulled back, making choking noises and coughing.

I half expected Josef to pursue her and make her try some more. But he seemed to accept that she couldn't do everything he wanted. He paused a moment and surveyed the rest of us. "Perhaps someone else would be better able to satisfy my needs," he murmured in his deep, sinister voice.

He looked directly at me. "Christina," he said slowly. "Christina—how about you?"

CHAPTER ELEVEN

I didn't hesitate. After all, I'd already given Josef oral sex once that day, and I'd enjoyed being able to make it feel so good that he couldn't resist me. So I walked forward, looking up at him expectantly. I stopped just in front of him with my hands clasped behind my back, and I waited.

"Kneel down, Christina," he told me.

I did as he told me, keeping my face composed, my posture straight and proud. I ignored everyone else watching me. I kept my attention strictly on Josef.

He moved forward and pressed the head of his cock to my lips. I kissed it, licked it, opened my mouth to it, and closed my eyes. Inch by inch, I felt his hot, hard flesh push in. His hands slid under my hair and around to the back of my neck. He linked his fingers there, so that I couldn't pull away—not that I had any intention of doing so.

I heard him give a little grunt of pleasure as he wiggled his hips from side to side, then thrust his cock in deeper. It nudged the back of my throat, and I shifted position slightly so that I could open myself to the entire length of him. He pressed in all the way—and I took it all, till every last inch of his cock was swallowed up.

He held himself there for a moment, enjoying the way I had engulfed him. Then, taking his time, he pulled back a little to allow me to breathe. And then he pressed forward again, still with his hands clasped behind my neck. His hot flesh slid deep; I took it all without resisting.

He started moving his hips in a slow but regular rhythm. I let his cock slide in and out, in and out, between my lips, across my tongue. I heard his breathing quicken. The tempo of his thrusts started speeding up. His hands clenched. His cock strained and pulsed, and I knew that in just a few seconds more he would come.

But evidently he didn't want that to happen just yet. Abruptly he let go of me and withdrew. His cock slid all the way out of my mouth; I opened my eyes and saw it sticking up rigid, bright pink, the veins bulging. It was so big, I congratulated myself for having taken the entire length of it so easily. Being slightly smashed on the wine had probably helped.

"Very good, Christina," Josef murmured. He stroked his fingers through my hair. "Very, very nice." He turned and stared at Jane. "You should be able to do as well. Maybe you just need some practice." He took her by the arm. "Here, I'm sure our musician friend won't object if you practice on him."

"Ow," Jane protested, flinching from Josef's grip on her arm. She flashed me a resentful look—I guess she was pissed at me for having made it all look so easy. Then she was hustled by Josef across to where Mark was sitting on a couple of giant pillows on the other side of the room.

"Kneel in front of Mr. Bernstein, and pull his shorts down," Josef told her. "Quickly, now!"

Jane got down on her knees. Her torn leotard ripped a little further, allowing both her breasts to fall out. They were fat and round, pure white with very large pale-pink nipples. She crossed her arms over them in embarrassment and looked up at Mark.

"Jane," Josef said warningly. "Do as I said."

Reluctantly she reached for Mark's boxer shorts. He was watching her as if he wasn't sure how to handle this situation. But when she tugged at his shorts, he didn't try to stop her. He lifted his hips and let her pull the shorts down to his ankles. His cock was revealed lying against his thigh. It was already half erect.

Jane took one last look at Josef, and saw he wasn't going to change his mind. So she grasped Mark's cock gently in her left hand, lowered her head, and started sucking him.

Mark smiled slowly. He was pretty drunk, but it didn't seem to affect his ability to get a hard-on. This must be a scene he'd been in often enough before— casual sex with a crowd of people, groupies giving head to their rock-musician idols. And of course I'd been in group scenes often enough myself. I wasn't so sure about Michel, Elizabeth, and Alexandra, though.

Those three were sticking together, standing in a little group in another corner of the room. Josef swaggered over to them, his black silk gown rippling as he walked. His cock was no longer sticking out as rigid as before, but it was still visible, large and swollen beneath a mat of black pubic hair, between the left and right edges of his robe.

"Elizabeth," Josef said slowly, studying the woman and smiling as if at a private joke. "Elizabeth, I think it would be nice for Jane if you go and stimulate her a little, while she practices her skills on Mr. Bernstein."

Elizabeth's eyes flashed as she glared at Josef and then glanced across the room at Jane sucking insistently on Mark's cock.

"Elizabeth," Josef repeated. He took her chin between

finger and thumb and tilted her head up. He stared into her eyes.

I don't know what she saw in his face, but it was enough to make her mind up for her. She jerked her jaw free of Josef's grasp, turned haughtily, and walked across to Jane with as much dignity as she could manage. I guessed she decided it was easier to give in than suffer the humiliation of being publicly spanked, as Jane had been.

"I want to see you suck Jane's nipples," Josef told her. "And touch her clitoris. I'm sure she'll like that." He turned to Alexandra. "You, my dear Alexandra. I remember seeing you in a passionate embrace with Christina last night. Of course, you may not remember it as clearly as I do." He grinned, and I saw him look down at Alexandra's small-breasted but firm-fleshed, lissome body. "Anyhow—why don't you go over to Christina now, and do some more of what you did so well with her before?"

Alexandra shrugged. "Sure," she said. She turned and came over to me, smiling as if to say, What the hell?

I took her hand in mine and squeezed. She returned the pressure. Then, without any embarrassment, she pulled me close to her and kissed me on the mouth.

Her hands caressed me down the sides of my neck. She moved her body and squirmed against me and I felt the warmth and smoothness of her skin. Her touch was very light, very sure, very arousing. She didn't need any aphrodisiac gas to get interested in my body—she was obviously bisexual.

She kissed around the curve of my jaw and started nibbling on my earlobe. "Chris?" she whispered, in between nibbles. "Chris, you got to teach me sometime how to give blowjobs like that." And she giggled.

I smiled despite myself. "Thanks for the compliment," I murmured. I ran my hand down her back and squeezed her ass. "But there's nothing to it. All you have to do is want to get out of this place very, very badly—and realize Josef's the guy who'll decide whether or not to let you."

Alexandra kissed me on the lips, then ran just the tip of her tongue up the side of my neck to my other ear. "All right for you," she whispered. "But where's my guy? Where's Carl, the little creep? He's the one I ought to be working on."

"Probably balling his sister," I murmured. Then I noticed Josef was watching us closely. "No more talk," I told Alexandra. "I think our commune leader wants action."

Straightaway Alexandra responded. She pushed her hands down inside my leotard, pulled my breasts up and out, and started kissing them. Her full, soft lips closed around first one nipple and then the other, and she sucked and worried them with her tongue till I felt myself getting tingly and wet inside. Slowly I sank down onto some cushions.

"I'll be there in a minute with both of you," Josef said, obviously enjoying the exhibition we were giving him. "But first—" He turned to Michel. "My Swiss friend, you have a remarkable choice, here. Four women, all of them soft and sensuous and available to you." He clapped his hand down on Michel's shoulder. "Which one of them do you want to fuck?"

I saw Michel scowl. I knew he was rebelling inside, much more than the rest of us. That was probably why Josef had left him till last.

Josef waited a moment, studying Michel. The Swiss skier refused to look Josef in the eye.

"Don't you like girls?" Josef said, lowering his voice—but there was still an edge to it. "Is that the problem? Have we made a mistake with you, Michel? Are you a faggot?''

I winced at the expression of suppressed rage on Michel's face. He clenched his fists and I saw a muscle tense at the side of his neck. But still he said nothing and remained standing staring rigidly ahead.

Josef sighed. ''I was hoping you would not give me this kind of trouble,'' he murmured. ''I want you to go over there, right now, to Elizabeth. I want you to lay her out on some of these pillows, and go down on her. Lick her clitoris. Push your tongue up inside her. Do that, Michel.''

The Swiss swallowed hard. He shook his head. ''No.'' he said.

Josef paused. He was the taller of the two, and more heavily muscled, and I thought he could probably win any fight with Michel. But there was no mistaking Michel's intention to resist. It could get messy.

''Very well,'' Josef said. ''For now, you will watch. We will deal with you later.'' And he turned his back and came over to where I still was with Alexandra— who by this time was kissing my belly and on her way down to my crotch.

I wondered if Michel was surprised by Josef backing away from a confrontation. But it was impossible to read Michel's face. He stood impassively, watching our group-sex scene as if it meant nothing to him.

Josef paused beside me. He didn't look as if he felt defeated by Michel's obstinacy. In fact, he looked pleased with himself. I wondered what he planned to do to persuade the Swiss to join the party.

''Christina,'' Josef said, interrupting my speculations. ''You and Alexandra, here, will take turns making love to me.'' He kicked a couple of cushions against the wall, sat down with his back against them, and opened his robe. He reached for his cock and held it up, clasped firmly in his fist. "First, you will both use your lips and tongues," he said.

I glanced at Alexandra. She met my eyes for a moment, smiled and shrugged almost imperceptibly. She seemed to be saying, What have we got to lose?

I stretched out on one side of Josef, making myself comfortable. Alexandra followed my example on the other side of him. We both started kissing his cock. Our mouths touched as we reached the head of it. I wriggled my tongue over the tip, tasting the saltiness. Alexandra's tongue touched mine. Our faces were only an inch apart, and I felt the softness of her cheek as it brushed against my face for a moment. Her breath was a warm caress. When I stroked my fingers along the length of Josef's penis, my hand slid over Alexandra's. It was a very, very intimate scene.

"Kiss each other," I heard Josef's voice commanding us. We hardly needed to be told. I kept hold of Josef in one hand, rubbing my fingers gently up and down to keep him aroused. Then I diverted most of my attention to Alexandra, who kissed me deeply and with passion. Her mouth was wonderfully soft and willing as her tongue crept between my lips. While she kissed me deep and long, I felt her reach out and rub her fingertips over the nipple of my left breast.

"Now suck my cock, Alexandra," said Josef. "While you, Christina, kiss my balls."

Reluctantly we broke our kiss. I was highly aroused, now, and getting more turned on all the time by the press of flesh against flesh. I wriggled around between Josef's legs and started eagerly kissing the underside of his cock, down to his balls. Meanwhile, just above me, Alexandra started sucking him busily. Her head bobbed up and down as her lips made wet noises.

"A little slower," Josef told her. He was watching us through half-closed eyes, reclining like a lord. "And take it deeper, Alexandra. As deep as you can. Yes. Suck hard, now. Hard. Ahhhh. . . . Very good. Not quite as good as your friend Christina, but very good.'' He grunted and shifted his hips. ''Keep on doing it like that.'' I felt his body shift as he turned to look across the room. ''Elizabeth! Come here. And you, Jane.''

I kept on caressing and kissing Josef's balls, since I had not been told to stop. Then I felt his fingers tugging at my hair. I lifted my head from between his legs and looked up at him.

''Christina, you will stand just behind Alexandra,'' he told me. ''Are you feeling aroused?''

I nodded. ''Very.''

''Good,'' he said. ''Touch yourself between your legs, just enough to stay aroused.'' He turned and looked as Jane and Elizabeth walked over to us. ''You, Mark,'' he called to the musician, lying stretched out with a big hard-on where Jane had been sucking him. ''You join us here, too. I want you all here, all around me. All of you, my—my family, here. All of you will now do your part to give me pleasure.''

CHAPTER TWELVE

A couple of minutes later, after Josef had given instructions to us, this is how it looked: Alexandra lay between his legs, still using her mouth on him. Her rich auburn hair hung half-concealing her face as she moved her head up and down, sucking insistently. Beside her Elizabeth was caressing Josef's chest, running her fingernails lightly across his tanned skin and through the tight curls of black body hair. Jane, meanwhile, knelt beside Josef where he could reach out and caress and play with her ample tits. And I was still touching myself, fingering my clitoris and running my fingers across my nipples. He watched me avidly, simultaneously enjoying the attentions of Alexandra and Elizabeth while clutching Jane's breasts in his big hands.

The only person unaccounted for was Mark. He stood watching, his cock still hard, and seemed to be getting off on the spectacle.

But Josef had plans for him, too. "Mark," he said. Josef was so aroused by what was happening that he seemed to find it difficult to speak. He sounded out of breath. "Mark, go to Christina." He pointed to me. "Christina. I want to watch you go down on Mark." He grunted and closed his eyes for a moment, savoring the waves of pleasure. I watched him dig his fingers deep into Jane's soft, heavy breasts. Then he got control of himself, stopping himself from reaching orgasm.

He opened his eyes and looked at me again. "Go on, Christina. Suck him."

My oral talents were certainly in demand, I thought to myself. Maybe Josef had a hangup about it. Maybe that was his big weakness. If so, I certainly knew how to exploit it.

Mark stood watching me while I knelt and started sucking his cock. I didn't fool around with any preliminaries—I took hold of his penis and swallowed the whole length of it in one quick movement. Then I braced myself by holding onto his hips and I began moving my head quickly to and fro.

Watching me seemed to be the last stimulus that Josef needed. His breathing became labored. He grunted and twisted. "Faster," he muttered to Alexandra, who was still working on him busily. He curled his fingers, digging them into Jane's tits until she gave a little cry. He ignored her, holding the soft flesh in a fierce grip. "Elizabeth, kiss my chest," he commanded. She moved to obey. He continued staring straight at me, and as I went on sucking Mark I managed to watch him. I moved my head faster, making busy wet noises. My long blond hair danced around my face. Mark gasped—he was almost coming.

"Yes," I heard Josef say. He clenched his jaw. His lips pulled back from his teeth as his muscles tightened in his chest and arms. He arched his back and groaned and thrust his hips upward, pushing his cock deeper into Alexandra's mouth. "Yes!" he gasped. And then he came, his body writhing as he raked his fingernails across Jane's breasts. His bearded face contorted with an expression of fierce triumph.

Mark came in my mouth just a couple of seconds later. He shivered and gasped and clutched my head in his hands as I went on sucking as hard as I could, savoring the taste of his come and drinking it down.

In the aftermath of the men's orgasms, we all rested a moment. I was feeling extremely horny by this time, and I think the other three women were turned on too. We were still a little high from the wine, and the pressure of flesh on flesh, the sounds and the smells of sex, all made it hard not to be aroused. I could see that Jane's cheeks were flushed, and even Elizabeth looked excited.

Josef quickly regained his composure after his orgasm. He stood up and drew his robe around him. He looked at us all. "Good," he said. "Very good. But we will not stop now. You, Jane, and Elizabeth—since you both seem . . . interested . . . you should now please each other."

Jane looked at Elizabeth. She blushed and giggled. The mood had become a lot more relaxed, and I think all of us were beginning to realize that this situation didn't have to be totally grim—we could still have some fun. In fact, sex was a way of making ourselves forget the more difficult aspects of being prisoners in Josef's world.

Elizabeth reached out and toyed with one of Jane's breasts, then rubbed her finger and thumb over the nipple. "Shall we do what the man told us, honey?" she said.

"All right," said Jane. She hesitated, then leaned forward and kissed Elizabeth on the cheek. Elizabeth responded by grabbing hold of Jane's face and kissing her hard on the mouth. Something told me that the older woman was no stranger to bisexual scenes.

Jane seemed uncertain about the kiss at first, but soon started responding. Within a minute, the two women were stretched out facing each other side by side on the soft cushions in a passionate embrace. Elizabeth reached down and started playing with Jane's clitoris. Jane gasped and rolled onto her back, and opened her legs wide. Elizabeth worked two fingers into Jane's pussy and then took her hand away and replaced it with her mouth. She moved so that her legs were on either side of the girl, and then lowered herself till her muff pressed against Jane's face. Jane lifted her head and started doing for Elizabeth what Elizabeth was doing for her.

Josef went over to Mark, who was sitting watching the women's sex play. "Whenever you want to," Josef said to the musician, "you should join them. Take whichever woman you want." Then Josef turned back to me. "You, Christina, and you, Alexandra—I need both of you to assist me now."

I glanced at Alexandra, and at the same moment she looked at me. More sex with Josef? Was he insatiable? In which case, I hoped he'd pay some attention to our needs this time, instead of just his own. I had a powerful desire for an orgasm, and I sensed that Alexandra felt the same way.

But it turned out that that wasn't what Josef had in mind. "There is still a member of our group who refuses to join us," he said. He put one arm around Alexandra's shoulders and his other arm around mine. He was tall enough for my shoulder to fit easily under his armpit. I felt puny against the weight and strength of his body.

"You see our Swiss friend over there," Josef murmured to Alexandra and me. He nodded in the direction of Michel, who was sitting as far away as possible, studiously ignoring the rest of us. "I think it is time for us to . . . persuade him . . . that he is foolish to deny himself the pleasures that we have to offer. Wouldn't you agree?"

Well, neither Alexandra nor I was about to try to disagree. On the other hand, I wasn't too happy about the notion of getting Michel to join the party. He seemed the kind of guy who didn't change his mind easily, once it was made up. "I'm not sure if we can—" I began, looking up at Josef.

"Of course you can. How could he resist you, Christina? Or you, Alexandra." Keeping his arms around us, Josef started walking across the room. He gave us no choice but to walk with him.

We stopped just in front of Michel. "My Swiss friend," said Josef. "It is time for you to stop being so obstinate."

Michel looked at me and Alexandra, then at Josef. He folded his arms. "You have forced them to obey you. You have made them take part in your corrupt fantasies," he said to Josef. "But I will not."

I felt Josef's muscles tense in the arm that he had around me. I didn't like what was shaping up here—we could do without a fight between the two men. Still, I figured I had another chance here to make myself seem indispensable to Josef. So I spoke up before he could say anything more.

"Michel, we might as well enjoy ourselves," I said. I kept my voice light and playful. He looked at me, and I showed my body off to him blatantly, cradling my naked breasts and tilting my hips. I could tell that he obviously liked what he saw. But then he got himself back under control and deliberately looked away.

"I will not change my mind, Christina. We can only save ourselves if we refuse to cooperate. Passive resistance, I think you call it."

"You're fooling yourself," said Josef. "I've already proved to you that we have drugs here that can destroy any resistance and make you do whatever we want you to do. Why pretend you can defy me?"

Michel resolutely shook his head. "You can use whatever drugs you like, such as the gas you gave us last night. And then, I have no doubt, you can compel me to do what you want. But so long as I am in my right mind, you cannot break my will.''

Josef took his arms away from Alexandra and myself. He flexed his muscles. I could see that Michel's attitude was getting him angry. I'd already figured that Josef's main goal was to have us submit to his desires voluntarily, to enslave ourselves to him. He couldn't tolerate open defiance. So Michel's attitude was the worst possible.

I stepped quickly between the two men before the confrontation had a chance to escalate. I placed my hands gently on Michel's shoulders. ''Michel, this isn't the time and place to make a stand,'' I said softly. ''It doesn't make sense. Do you want to be locked away in your room, without any comforts or necessities? Why not cooperate, instead? After all''—I deliberately pressed the length of my naked body against him—''it might even be kind of fun.''

Michel closed his eyes. I was pleased to see that he was having trouble maintaining his cool. ''Do not do this, Christina,'' he said. His voice was tense.

I kissed him on the cheek and ran my fingertips down the side of his neck, down across his naked chest, down to the elastic of the boxer shorts he was wearing. ''Don't do what?'' I said, slipping my fingertips inside the shorts.

''No!'' he told me, grabbing my arm.

I rubbed my tits across his chest and kissed the side of his neck, nipping his skin in my teeth. ''Why not, Michel? Why not? We might as well, while we're here. For as long as we're prisoners.'' I nibbled the lobe of his ear. ''I want it,'' I whispered. ''I really want it, and I'd rather have it with you than with Josef. Honestly, I don't think I could stand having sex with him anymore. Please don't make me do that.''

I felt Michel weaken then. I only hoped Josef hadn't been able to hear what I said.

"Christina, we have to be strong," Michel complained. "We have to refuse this man. If we refuse, we are no use to him. Then he will let us go."

I ran my hands around behind his waist and pulled his hips to mine. I rubbed against him, slowly, persuasively. "If we resist, we'll get drugged again, or worse," I said. "Wouldn't you rather stay in your right mind?" I suddenly kissed him hard on the mouth. "Please, Michel."

He groaned and closed his eyes, and I knew I had him. I clung to him and kissed him some more. Then I boldly reached down and grabbed his cock inside his shorts, and started massaging it. I felt him begin to get hard. "Let's sit down," I whispered to him.

Reluctantly, he sat on the nearest pile of pillows. I pushed with my hands against his shoulders and made him lie down on his back. Then I glanced quickly at Alexandra, and beckoned her over. At the same time I noticed that Josef was watching with obvious pleasure. He had his hand inside his robe and was masturbating himself. I was right—the man really was insatiable.

I returned my attention to Michel. I kissed his mouth, his cheeks, his chest. I rolled the head of his cock gently between my finger and thumb. Then I licked the tips of my fingers and started rubbing them in little circles under the end of his cock where I knew it was most sensitive. He lay with his eyes shut, trying to resist what I was doing to him. But the size of his erection showed that his resistance was no longer very effective.

Alexandra joined me. "I'll go on hugging and kissing him," I whispered to her. "You get on him as soon as he's hard enough, all right?"

She nodded, and kissed me on the cheek.

I worked on Michel some more, and he began to respond despite himself. He opened his mouth when I kissed him. I thrust my tongue between his lips. I twined my fingers in his hair and kissed him fiercely. And all the while I continued stroking and rubbing his cock.

Finally I took my hand away. Alexandra quickly put her hand where mine had been. And she started easing his shorts off.

Michel reached instinctively to stop what was happening, but he was too slow and too clumsy. In just a couple of seconds Alexandra had him naked and was lowering herself astride him, guiding his cock up between her legs.

"No——" Michel began, but I smothered his objections with more kisses, deep and insistent and as erotic as I knew how.

Alexandra wriggled a little from side to side, worked the head of his cock between her labes, and then slowly sat down on him. His cock thrust up inside her, all the way. She braced herself with her hands on his hips and started fucking herself on him, gently at first but soon increasing the tempo. She had obviously gotten as horny as I had and was enjoying being in a dominant role now, persuading this man to give her the satisfaction she craved.

Michel started breathing faster. He opened his eyes and stared at me where I was still hugging him, my face close to his. "You should not have done this, Christina," he said. He swallowed hard. Then he reached out and ran his fingers over my lips and my cheeks.

I bent my head over his and kissed him some more. Behind me, I heard Alexandra gasping with excitememt now, bouncing up and down on Michel with abandon. I glanced around and was just in time to see her come. She threw her head back, opened her mouth, and let out a triumphant cry, jamming her hips down hard and grinding them to and fro while the waves of her orgasm rippled through her.

I waited for her excitement to subside, then gestured to her to switch places with me. Michel was still a ways from coming himself, and I wanted my share.

Alexandra smiled at me and got up off Michel. His cock came out of her, long and hard and wet. I quickly straddled it and sank it deep inside myself. It pushed up inside me, and I closed my eyes and savored the feeling. This was what I had been wanting. I settled my ass down on him, and his pelvic bone nudged against my clitoris. I wiggled my hips, and little shivers of pleasure radiated through me.

Meanwhile, Alexandra fell across Michel's chest, took his head in her hands, and started kissing him, taking up where I had left off. He made feeble attempts to resist, but I started moving quickly up and down on him, and his resistance once again died. I reached behind me and started playing with his balls and running my fingernails up and down the insides of his thighs. I felt him tense and arch his back. He closed his legs, trapping my hand there. I cupped his balls and held them while I continued fucking myself on him, increasing the tempo.

Then I felt a hand on my shoulder. I looked up, startled by the interruption. Josef was there, staring down at me. He smiled. His cock was once again fully erect, sticking out of his robe. He was fondling it gently. It didn't take me long to realize what he wanted.

I started sucking him while I was fucking myself on Michel. I closed my eyes and gave myself up to the erotic sensuality of the scene. Michel's cock was jammed deep inside my cunt, so long and hard I felt impaled on it. Josef's penis was stuffed deep into my mouth and throat, so fat and heavy I felt as if every inch of me was filled. I sucked him furiously, wriggling my tongue and working my lips around the swollen shaft. I jerked my hips up and down and to and fro on Michel, feeling my own excitement mount. The sensations rose in a crescendo. I forgot where I was. And then, in great spasms, I came.

The two men both came also, almost simultaneously. Michel's cock twitched and strained inside me and I felt the moist warmth of his come welling up. Josef's cock stiffened and spasmed and I tasted his semen for the second time that day and drank down the thick, salty mouthful.

Then Josef pulled out of my mouth, and I fell down upon Michel. I was gasping for breath, and he was breathing hard too. His face was red, and he had an expression of bewilderment at what had happened to him. For a moment I just lay there, with my cheek on his chest, and closed my eyes. I could hear my heart pounding inside my head. My whole body was tingling with the afterglow from my orgasm. A comfortable pleasure-ache spread out slowly across my belly from my vagina. I sighed with pleasure, feeling fully satisfied.

If this was what happened on just the first night of our stay in Josef's commune, I couldn't help wondering, what would the rest of our stay be like?

CHAPTER THIRTEEN

Michel pushed me away roughly. I was still dizzy and euphoric from the frantic sex I'd had with him and Josef. I fell off him and looked up in surprise as he grabbed his boxer shorts, stood up, and pulled them on with a furious look on his face.

"Hey," I called to him. "Was it that bad?"

He looked as if there were a dozen different things he wanted to say, but he held them all back. He glared at me, then glared at Josef, then marched off to a far corner of the room, sat down there, and stared pointedly away from us.

"Sooner or later, Michel will have to come to see that it is easier to cooperate than to fight," said Josef. He reached down and fondled my blond hair. "You were wonderful, my dear. You, and Alexandra. Both of you will be rewarded."

"Thanks," I said, looking up at him and trying to seem worshipful. I was lying near his feet; impulsively I bent over and kissed one foot, then the other. I hoped I wasn't being too corny, taking this submissive bit too far. But when I looked up again and saw the satisfaction on his face I knew I'd done the right thing.

"It is time for me to leave you now," Josef said. "Until tomorrow. Carl will now come and take you to your rooms. He pointed across the room at Elizabeth and Jane, still lying in the 69 position, with Mark lying behind Jane, fondling her big breasts and masturbating slowly with a dreamy look on his face. "You will tell them, Christina, that in a few minutes they must be ready to return to their rooms for the night."

"Sure," I agreed.

Josef bent down. He took my face in his hands and kissed me on the mouth. It was forceful and yet quite tender. And then, before I had time to decide what he was trying to convey to me, if anything, he stood up again, walked quickly out of the room, and locked the door behind him.

Alexandra came and sat down beside me. "Got to hand it to you, Chris," she said.

I turned and looked at her. Her hair was a mess and her leotard was torn. She looked pleased with herself, though. "What do you mean?" I asked.

She nodded in the direction of the door where Josef had just walked out. "You did great," she said. She put her lips to my ear. "You'll have him eating out of your hand inside of a week."

I laughed. "We'll see. Frankly—I don't know if I should admit this—but he kind of turns me on. It's a challenge to get through to a man like that. And he's such a big hunk, I'm enjoying the things that happen along the way."

"I just wish I knew what happened to Carl," said Alexandra. "I don't get it; he and his sister were in the orgy last night, weren't they? I mean, I can't remember anything clearly, but I thought—"

I nodded. "Me too. Maybe they played it safe tonight, staying clear in case we got out of hand, not being drugged this time around." I stood up. "I better sort out the scene over there." I walked over to Mark and the other two women.

* * *

A little later, Carl Stanowski came and took us back to our rooms one by one. He took Michel first. I'd expected the skier to resist, but he went willingly. He still avoided looking at any of us, though, and he didn't say a word.

Carl came over to me next. "Miss van Bell?" he said. "Please come to your room now. We need to have everyone in the group secured at night. Just for the first few days, until we understand each other better." He smiled a strange, twisted kind of smile, and stared at me through his wire-frame glasses. His attention shifted from my face to my body, and back up again. He made me feel creepy; I was glad he was Alexandra's target, and not mine.

I followed him out and along the passageway. "You missed all the fun just now," I told him.

He opened the door of my room. I noticed he used a big, complicated kind of key. "In here," he told me, not replying directly to what I'd said. "Josef wishes you to know," he went on, "that your willingness and cooperation this evening have earned you ninety points in credit. Is there anything you want?"

I almost laughed in his face, and told him to go stuff his credit points up his ass. But I had to bite back the impulse, the way I'd been biting back my natural fighting tendency all along. For the time being, I had to remind myself, these guys are in control. I had no choice but to play their game, unless I wanted to do a noble number like Michel and go in for passive resistance, and be punished for it.

I surveyed the room. "I'd like two blankets, a hairbrush, comb, toothbrush, and clock," I said. "Oh, and a washcloth. Can I have all that stuff?"

"Everything but the clock. There will be no clocks provided, not as yet."

"Why not?" I asked. Something about this mousy little guy made me come on strong and belligerent—

maybe because I knew he was the one who'd invented the various drugs that had been given to us.

He avoided my eye. "There will be no clocks provided," he repeated. "Josef has given instructions."

That last bit sounded like an afterthought, and I had a sudden intuition that Josef hadn't been the one to make the rule. Maybe this was just Carl's own sadistic little game with me. Maybe I should be nicer to the creep. And yet, I didn't think I could be sweet to both of them.

"All right," I said, "But there are enough of these—credit points—for the rest of the stuff."

"Almost precisely," Carl agreed. "The items will be brought to you."

I gave him what I hoped was a warm, sexy smile. "Thanks, Carl. May I call you Carl?"

He shuffled his feet. I got the impression he didn't want to be here and was anxious to leave. "It is quite acceptable for you to use my first name, yes," he said. "And now—"

"No, just a moment," I said. I'd noticed the way he avoided looking directly at my nakedness; so I had a sudden perverse desire to flaunt it. "My skin's kind of dry," I told him, rubbing my hands down across my breasts. Actually my skin was fine, but I figured he had no way of knowing that. "You see where I mean?" I asked, cupping my left breast in my hand and pushing it up toward him. "Right here. You wouldn't have any kind of skin cream in this place, would you?"

He was obviously uncomfortable now. He readjusted his spectacles and continued trying not to look at me, although with me standing right in front of him that wasn't easy. "I'll see what I can do, Miss van Bell."

"*Christina*," I told him, reaching out and touching his arm. "We're all going to be seeing a lot of each other, right?"

He took a deep breath. "I would remind you, Miss van Bell, we are in charge here, not you." He scowled at me. "Now, I have a lot of other matters to attend to."

"Yes—but there's just one more thing—about my friend Alexandra? You know, the tall one with the dark brown hair?"

"What is it?" He went on scowling at me, but I could tell he was feeling ambivalent. He only half wanted to leave. I wondered what his hang-up was. Was he under orders from Josef not to molest me?

"I just wanted to tell you," I improvised, "Alexandra was kind of surprised that you didn't join the party this evening. I think she thinks you're kind of an interesting guy."

There was a moment's silence. Carl Stanowski studied me as if trying to decide if I were putting him on. I stared straight back at him and didn't move a muscle.

Finally he seemed to figure I might actually be telling the truth. "Thank you, Miss van Bell," he said. "I must leave you now." He nodded to me curtly, turned, and left my room, locking the door behind him.

I paused for a moment, wondering if I'd done the right thing. Well, why not? If Alexandra wanted to work on the guy, it wouldn't hurt to have him thinking she was interested in him. As far as I could tell, he had so many inhibitions, she'd be able to really get under his skin, if she had the chance to loosen him up a little. That kind of uptight guy would be hit hard if he once got it into his head that she had a crush on him.

Maybe he knew his own weaknesses, though. Maybe he only allowed himself to get intimate with women when he was strictly in control—like on the previous night, when we were under the influence of the aphrodisiac gas. I was sure he'd been part of the orgy that time. Tonight, however, he'd stayed away. And here in my room he'd tried to avoid even looking at my body, let alone touching me.

I decided I couldn't wait for a washcloth. I had to take a shower right away. So I went into the bathroom and cleaned myself up as thoroughly as I could. There was no shampoo, just a single bar of soap; I had to use that on my hair. Maybe if I was super-nice to Josef the next day I could get shampoo and a hair drier, too. I grimaced at having to think like that, but there it was: I didn't like being deprived of creature comforts.

When I came out of the shower I found that the items I'd asked for had been dumped on my bed. I went and tried my door, just in case the person who'd left the things had been careless. But of course he hadn't been.

I spread the blankets over the sheets that were already on the bed. Then I lay down. I realized I'd forgotten to ask for a pillow—that, too, would have to come tomorrow.

And then, before I was ready for it, the light suddenly dimmed to a faint glow and the room was plunged into semidarkness. Just enough for the TV camera to see by, I guessed.

I rolled over and went to sleep.

CHAPTER FOURTEEN

That night I dreamed I was back in Los Angeles with my lover Gary. We were cruising slowly along Mulholland Drive in his Mercedes 450SL through the soft, warm California night. I dreamed of the road snaking along the ridge overlooking the broad sweep of the valley spangled with lights. I dreamed I could smell the lush vegetation, I could hear the crickets, and I could feel the air blowing on my face through the open windows of the car, feel it wafting over me and caressing my body through the thin silk blouse I was wearing. It was so very real, I never doubted for a moment that I was there.

The caresses of the night wind were making me aroused. The silk fluttering across my nipples made them tingle and glow with an inner warmth. I could feel myself getting excited inside. I could feel the sensual need growing.

I moved closer to Gary and ran my fingernails lightly down the back of his neck, then caressed him around his ear and under the line of his jaw. I saw him turn and smile at me, his face outlined for a moment by the headlights of a passing car. He was so blond and handsome, so desirable, and he was mine. Knowing that was like an aphrodisiac.

I reached between his legs. He was wearing thin, tight pants. I ran my fingers lightly across his crotch and felt the presence of his cock just under the thin fabric.

He took hold of my wrist, and for a moment I thought he was trying to stop me; but then I realized he was pulling my hand harder against him.

So I started massaging him between the legs, slowly and deliberately, while we continued along the winding highway, with the warm night air blowing gently into the car. I felt his cock grow larger, pulsing and stiffening under my touch. I clutched at him, kneading him, loving the way I could arouse him so quickly.

I felt for the tag of the zipper and gradually eased it open. I slid my hand in and ran my fingers over his underpants. Then I found my way inside them and started touching his bare flesh.

This time, he tried to stop me. "Later, Chris," I heard him whisper. He attempted to pull my hand away.

But at this point I was too horny to stop. I pulled his cock out of his fly and held the hot, hard length of him in my hand. I closed my fingers around it and started masturbating him slowly, gently, insistently. "Don't you want it?" I murmured to him, moving closer so that my lips almost touched his ear and he could smell my perfume and feel my breath and the tantalizing touch of my blond hair against his neck.

"You know I want it. I always want it with you. But—"

I ignored the "but." I rubbed my fingers across the head of his cock, where it was moist. I tickled the underside of the shaft. I caressed his balls, working my fingers down through his pubic hair.

"No, Chris!" he told me, but his voice sounded plaintive, as if he knew there was nothing he could do to stop me.

I smiled to myself. I took one of his hands off the steering wheel and pressed it against me. I wasn't wearing a bra, and the shape of my flesh was obvious through the thin silk blouse. I felt his cock stiffen and grow still larger as I kept hold of his hand and closed his fingers around the swelling of my breast.

He made a little groaning noise. He was beginning to have trouble steering the car. "Pull off the road," I murmured to him.

"But we're late," he objected. "We have to—"

"We don't have to do anything we don't want to do," I told him. "Look, just ahead there—we can take that dirt road behind the trees."

He hit the brake. I knew he couldn't resist me, and knowing it made me want him even more. The car bumped over the curb, onto the dry grass and along the road I had seen. Bushes scraped along the sides of the car as we pulled out of sight of the highway. The hillsides were too steep for houses to be built along here— it was undeveloped land. But through the windshield we could still see the great panorama of the lights of the valley, shimmering in the heat-haze.

The car stopped and I brushed my lips lightly across Gary's cheek. He turned his head and his lips searched for mine. I held back for a moment, tantalizing him with more little kisses around his mouth and chin. And then I let him kiss me and opened my mouth wide as his tongue searched for mine. His fingers clenched on my breasts and then started unbuttoning my blouse. I arched my back and tensed as I felt him slide his hands inside and clutch at my nakedness. He caressed my nipples, and a tingling warmth spread across the front of my body and down to my crotch.

I was still touching his cock, and started masturbating him faster with urgent little motions of my hand. I felt his flesh throbbing in rhythm with his heartbeats.

He moved his hands up to my face and touched my cheeks, my forehead, the line of my jaw. "You're so beautiful, Chris," he whispered. "So damned beautiful." He let out a little gasp as I moved my fingers back to the top of his cock and tickled it insistently. "Chris, I want you," he said.

"Then let's recline the seats," I whispered to him.

He did as I suggested. Quickly I pulled my legs up, squirmed around, and moved astride him. I lay on him, then, with my naked breasts squashed against his chest. I kissed him very hard and squirmed so that my body rubbed to and fro across him. My hair fell down around his face. My mouth was constantly on his, while my fingers once again found his cock. I pulled up my skirt, guided him between my thighs, then closed them around him and moved my hips so that the soft skin held his cock and rubbed it tantalizingly.

"You want to fuck me?" I whispered to him. "You want me to let you inside?"

"You know I do. You know I can't resist you, Chris."

I reached down and toyed with him. I drummed the tips of my fingers lightly across the head of his penis. "I don't know if I'm ready, Gary," I told him playfully.

He pushed his hand down between our bodies and I felt his fingers slide up between my legs. He pushed one finger between my labes, then another.

He found how wet I was and grinned at me. "You feel ready enough to me," he murmured.

I tried to pull his hand away, but he kept it there. His finger found my clitoris and played with it gently, persuasively. I felt a great warm wave sweep through me. I had to have him. I had to feel his cock thrusting into me.

I grabbed his head in my hands, twining my fingers in his curly blond hair. I kissed him fiercely. Then I reached down, took hold of his cock, and guided it between my labes. I lowered my hips and he pushed into me, a little at first, then deeper, so very deep.

I sat up on him, bracing myself with my hands on his shoulders. His hands clutched at my naked tits. He groaned and twisted under me.

I let my head fall back so that I could feel my own hair tickling my naked shoulders. I moved my buttocks in little circles, savoring the presence of his cock inside my body. I felt him struggling to move under me, and I realized I didn't want to tantalize him any longer.

"You really want me, Gary?" I whispered to him. I undid a couple of buttons of his shirt and slid my fingers inside. I raked my nails gently across his chest. "You really, really want me?"

"You know it," he said. "You've always known it."

"All right, then," I said. Keeping him inside me, I let myself fall slowly to the left, easing myself down until he and I were lying side by side, my legs wrapped around him, my breasts almost touching his chest.

He started moving quickly, eagerly. His hips made impatient thrusts. He held my face and gave me a dozen fleeting kisses. He moved his hands down to my tits and felt them as if discovering them, exploring them for the first time, savoring every contour, every nuance of the flesh. His breathing came very fast, in little gasps. He looked at me as if I were so lovely he could hardly believe he was having me. It was wonderful; his adoration was like a drug. I felt so desirable, so beautiful. I opened myself to him totally. I took him as deep as he could go.

His thrusts speeded up even more, into a frenzy. He reached between my legs and his fingers touched where he was fucking me, then moved up to my clitoris.

I gasped and trembled at the sudden sensations. It was almost too intense to bear. He rolled my clitoris to and fro, and I heard myself moan and cry. I clutched at him, kissed him, gave myself to him. His hips pounded against me as our bodies made wet noises, squirming together on the car seats. I felt myself quiver inside, and then all the dams broke and I came in great spasms. I held Gary in a desperate embrace as the orgasm surged through me.

Then he came too, grunting and gasping and groaning and clutching me to him. His cock seemed to swell and strain, and then I felt it jerk and spurt inside me. It seemed to go on and on forever.

We rested in each other's arms. Our breathing slowed. I kissed Gary's face. "Gary," I began to say, "Gary, I—"

But before I could tell him how much I cared for him, and how wonderful it had all felt for me, my vision wavered. A bright light shone down on us from somewhere. In my dream I turned around, startled, thinking maybe a police patrol had found us. But then I felt the dream slipping away, and I realized that I wasn't really with Gary in Los Angeles at all; it had just been an erotic fantasy. I tried to hold onto the vividness of the car interior and my lover in my arms, but it dissolved, and I opened my eyes and found myself in my little cubicle in Josef's hideaway. They had turned the lights back up to full intensity—that was why I had dreamed of the night becoming floodlit. I blinked in the sudden glare from the ceiling fixture.

I found that the covers had fallen off the bed and I was lying there naked. My hand was between my legs, I was wet inside, and my skin was flushed. I'd been touching myself in my sleep. That part had been real—the surge of erotic feelings, and my orgasm.

I felt a sudden sense of melancholy. I remembered my lovemaking with Gary on the morning Helen Stanowski had turned up at my house and kidnapped me. I realized I had pushed thoughts of Gary out of my mind, in order to cope with the new situation I found myself in. But I missed him terribly.

I pulled my hand away from my pussy and turned quickly as I heard a key in the lock of the door of my cubicle. I suddenly felt horribly naked and exposed.

The door swung open, and Carl Stanowski stood there, studying me with his shifty eyes behind his wire-framed spectacles. I saw him take in every inch of my nakedness.

The previous night, I had been ready to flaunt myself to him. But now, with visions of Gary still fresh in my imagination, all I wanted to do was hide my body from this man. I drew up my knees and hugged them against my breasts. "What do you want?" I demanded.

Carl stood on the doorway watching me for a moment more. Then he pulled something from the pocket of the white doctor's coat that he was wearing. He threw the item to me.

Instinctively, I caught it. It was the jar of skin cream that I had asked for the previous night.

"Perhaps you will need some help in applying the ointment to your dry skin?" Carl said. He gave me a thin smile which was almost a sneer. Last night, somehow I'd had him on the defensive. This morning, he felt much more sure of himself—and suddenly I knew why.

"Were you watching me while I was asleep?" I asked him. I felt myself getting angry. I pointed up at the TV camera, beside the light, behind the glass panel in the ceiling. "Is that how you get your sick kicks? Spying on people?"

He didn't reply. He just stood there with his weird, distasteful smile. He rattled his bunch of keys. "You may join your other friends in the communal room, Miss van Bell,'' he said, finally. ''Breakfast will be available.''

He took one last look at my nakedness, and then he walked away without another word.

CHAPTER FIFTEEN

I dressed myself in one of the leotards that I found stored in the little bureau of my room. I washed my face and brushed my hair. I wished I had some makeup to put on; maybe I could get Josef to give me some, if I was a good girl. I grimaced at the thought of once again having to play that role to earn my rewards.

Carl had left the door of my cubicle unlocked and standing open a few inches. I went and peered out into the passageway. Then I stepped out and walked along the passageway to the cubicle next to mine. Its door was open too. I peeked inside and found Alexandra checking her appearance in a hand mirror. "Hi," I said to her. "Are we being allowed to look after ourselves this morning?"

She turned and saw me and her face lit up with a big smile. She ran across and gave me a hug. Then she kissed me hard on the mouth. "Chris, it's so good to see you!" she exclaimed.

I tried to hold back a little—I wasn't sure I wanted her developing some kind of a crush on me. I was beginning to wonder if she was the kind of bisexual woman who was only interested in men for practical reasons, and turned to women when she needed love and affection. "How are you this morning?" I asked her.

She shrugged. "It was a rough night—I have a lot to

tell you—but what's this with the open-door policy?"
She let go of me and went out into the hallway.

We quickly found that the other cubicles had also
been unlocked, and our fellow prisoners were emerging
one by one. Including Robert French: He stumbled out
of his little room looking confused and disoriented, his
skin sunburned bright red, his legs still covered in
scratches and swollen from insect bites.

"Robert!" I exclaimed. "Robert, are you all right?"

He saw me a seemed to take a moment to focus and
remember who I was. He frowned. "I'm . . . just . . .
fine," he said slowly.

He didn't seem fine at all. He looked as though he'd
been lobotomized. I went up to him and felt his forehead; his temperature was normal, though nothing else
about him seemed to be. "What did they do to you?" I
asked. "Did they drug you, or what?"

He shook his head slowly. "I—can't remember. I
was very dizzy. From the sun." He hesitated. "Carl
Stanowski saved my life, you know," he added vaguely. Then he turned and walked away from me.

Well, I thought, maybe he'd get himself back together
if we left him alone for a while. I glanced around. All
my other companions had emerged into the hallway—
with a single exception: Michel seemed to be still locked
in.

We banged on the one remaining locked door, and
shouted. There was a very, very faint response. The
doors were so thick and so well soundproofed that any
real communication was out of the question. I shrugged.
"That's what he gets in exchange for his passive resistance," I said. "Solitary confinement."

"And no breakfast," added Mark. "When Carl opened
your door this morning, didn't he say something about
food in the orgy room?"

"That's right," I agreed. "Guess we're allowed to

take care of ourselves today—those of us who obeyed orders last night.''

"Yeah," said Mark, looking disgusted. "This whole scene is really beginning to bring me down. You know?" He turned and walked along the corridor and through the door at the end, into the communal room. The others followed him.

I held Alexandra's arm. "Just a second. We may as well make sure that there's been no mistake." I led her back along the corridor in the opposite direction, to the main access door, through which we had originally been brought to the basement.

The door was solid steel encased in a steel frame, with an impressive-looking lock on it, and no handle. Obviously, it opened inward. I tried prying at the edge of it and succeeded only in breaking a fingernail. "Guess they didn't make a mistake after all," I said to Alexandra with a wry smile. "We're free to roam around today, as long as we stay stuck down here in the basement." I sighed. "So let's go eat, before the others get it all."

It turned out that breakfast was like all the other meals: sandwiches of cold ham and turkey, some canned fruit, and a choice of water or wine. Also, there was a big plastic bottle of multivitamins. Evidently Josef intended his commune to be totally self-sufficient, which meant no supplies of fresh fruit or vegetables. I wondered how long his food reserves would last: a month? Two months?

We sat around nibbling at the dull food. "I hope you had a comfortable night, my dear," Elizabeth said to me. She had a catty tone in her voice which I couldn't quite figure out.

"It was all right," I answered cautiously.

"You were warm enough, were you?"

"Yes," I said without thinking, "though I needed both blankets."

She smiled nastily. "Mmmm, I'm sure they kept you warm. And this morning you enjoyed the use of a hairbrush, right? Tell me, my dear, did they give you any other little goodies?"

Now I understood. I saw her hair in tangles, and realized Josef hadn't been quite so generous about handing out rewards to her. And she was just the type to make a scene out of it. "Surely you were given—" I began.

"One blanket, and not another goddamned thing," she said in a sharp, angry voice. She turned to Jane. "What about you, sweetie?"

Jane flinched. I noticed she was sitting near Mark. She glanced at him as if for reassurance. "I got a few things," she said meekly.

"I'm sure you did. What about the rest of you?" She turned to each of us in turn.

It quickly became apparent that all of us had received more than Elizabeth—even Robert French, though he still seemed to have some trouble describing anything that had happened to him, and still spoke slowly and clumsily as if he were on drugs, which, I realized, he probably was. It was creepy seeing this violent, angry man turned into some kind of walking zombie.

"So why the hell is it me who gets shortchanged?" Elizabeth demanded. "Why does that bastard pick on me? Didn't I do everything he wanted? Didn't I?"

I stood up and walked over to her. I put my hand on her shoulder. "He probably did this just to get you riled up," I murmured to her. "Don't let it get to you. It's just a game. Part of his power trip."

She shook my hand away and glared at me. "And you love it, right? Don't play innocent, honey. I saw how you fawned over him. You couldn't get enough of it, could you? You'd do just about anything, wouldn't you?'' She looked at me as if I were dirt.

I hesitated, realizing that Josef might be listening in on our conversation at that very moment. ''I'll gladly loan you my hairbrush, and anything else,'' I said, trying to keep my voice sounding reasonable. At the same time, even as I made the offer, I felt reluctant about it. What if Elizabeth refused to return the things I loaned her?

I thought it through further and realized this, too, was part of Josef's scheme. He wanted us to be suspicious of each other and hoard the items he gave us. The distribution was deliberately unfair, to stir up resentment in the group and keep us divided against each other instead of united against him. I wanted to say all this, but if Josef was listening in, I didn't want him to know that I knew. I had to maintain my role as his dumb, devoted lover.

Elizabeth turned away from me. ''I'll never use anything of yours,'' she told me in a tone of disgust.

''Hey, cool it,'' said Mark. ''I mean, what's the big deal? We can all share our shit, right?'' He looked hopefully from face to face.

''Right,'' Jane agreed with him. But no one else spoke up.

''I need the things they gave me,'' said Robert French, slowly and awkwardly, like an autistic child. His face crumpled as if he were going to burst into tears. ''Don't take them away from me. I won't let you take them away.''

''Jesus Christ, man, I can't deal with this,'' said Mark. He put his face in his hands.

Alexandra went over to Robert. She put her arm around his shoulders. ''It's all right, no one's going to steal your things,'' she murmured to him. ''Really, it's all right. Tell you what—why don't we go back to your room right now, so you can see that nothing's been touched?''

French nodded. "Yes. I would like that," he said.

Alexandra helped him to his feet. I went over and joined her, and together we walked French out of the room—anything to get him out of sight, so we wouldn't have to sit there watching him acting like a travesty of himself. We took him to his cubicle, closed the door, and returned to the communal room.

"I need a drink," Mark then said. He grabbed one of the bottles and poured himself a cup.

So far, no one else had touched the wine—it seemed much too early for that. But now, I realized, I didn't mind blurring reality a little. I could see that the others felt the same way, that if we stayed trapped in this place for very long we'd all become alcoholics.

"I wonder if they'll give us anything to do during the day," Alexandra said, taking the bottle from Mark and pouring some for herself. "I mean, it can't be sex all the time, day and night. And there aren't enough chores, like cleaning up the place. All the cups and plates are paper, and the knives and forks are plastic—"

"So we can't stab that son of a bitch in the throat," Elizabeth put in. She still had a mean, angry look on her face.

"This room is probably wired for sound," Alexandra interrupted her.

"So what?" said Elizabeth. "You think that bastard doesn't know that we all hate his guts? You think it's news to him that if any one of us had the chance, we'd castrate him?" She suddenly turned on me. "All except our glamour girl, here. You wouldn't want to do that, would you, honey? You'd rather suck it than cut it off. Right?"

I took a deep breath and tried to keep my anger under

control. "For an elegant lady, you have a foul mouth," I told her.

"A foul mouth?" she snapped back. "You ought to be the expert on that. After having him come in it yesterday."

I decided the only way to cope with her was to outdo her own vulgarity. "It was delicious," I told her. "I savored every last drop." I gave her a sweet smile. "That's probably why I'm so good at it," I added. "And that's why I was given all the little luxuries I wanted."

I stopped then, realizing I'd gone much too far. The wine was already working on me, and all the frustrations of being trapped in the basement were welling up. I was venting them on Elizabeth, which wasn't wise.

But it was too late to smooth things over. She stood up and marched over to me. "You filthy little whore," she said. And then she spat in my face.

No one had ever done that to me. It was a horrible sensation, and I rubbed my hand and arm furiously across my cheek. But that just transferred Elizabeth's spittle from one part of my skin to another. She had made me suddenly unclean, and I loathed her for it. I stood up, trembling.

"I'm warning you," I said, keeping my voice as level as I could. "I can hurt you, so you'd better keep your distance from now on."

She looked straight into my eyes, and I could see she was pleased with herself for having gotten me riled. She smirked. "All you others just hear how she threatened me?" she said. "You cheap little slut," she added. And then, very quickly, she slapped my face.

I grabbed her wrist and twisted it. I went on twisting till her arm was up behind her back.

Suddenly other hands grabbed me. "Leave her alone,

Chris!'' I heard Alexandra shouting at me. "What the hell has gotten into you?"

Then Mark was pulling at me, and Jane was trying to put herself between me and Elizabeth. But I was so mad I wouldn't let go. I wanted to vent all my anger on someone or something, and Elizabeth had given me the perfect excuse.

But soon a new voice was added to the others—Josef's voice. "Let her go, Christina," he said calmly, but in a commanding tone. He was standing in the doorway— he'd been watching us from there for the last couple of minutes.

He walked slowly toward me. "Let her go. If you two have some kind of disagreement, I can think of some much more interesting ways to settle it." And he grinned as if at some cruel private joke.

CHAPTER SIXTEEN

Josef took me by the shoulder and firmly held me to one side. Reluctantly, I let go of Elizabeth. "I'm sorry, Josef," I said, trying to sound genuinely contrite. "She got me mad, and—"

"You threatened me!" Elizabeth interrupted. "Josef, didn't you hear her threaten me?"

Josef looked at us both with supercilious amusement, like a schoolteacher dealing with two bitchy little schoolgirls. "You will both be quiet," he commanded us.

There was a moment's silence. "But—" Elizabeth began.

Josef turned to her. He took her by her upper arm, and I saw his hand clench it as Elizabeth winced. "You will be quiet, Elizabeth," he told her.

She nodded dumbly, and all the fight went out of her. She stared up at him apprehensively.

Josef nodded, acknowledging her acquiescence. He was wearing his black robe again and looked bright-eyed, fresh, and alert. His beard seemed newly trimmed. His thick black hair was neatly combed; it glistened as he moved.

He glanced around at Mark, Jane, and Alexandra. "You will sit," he told them. "And Alexandra, you are quite correct. I am always able to overhear what is said in this room, and elsewhere. It is necessary for me to know everything that goes on here. Otherwise there is always a chance that something . . . bad . . . might happen between my commune members. I'm sure you understand." He turned back to Elizabeth. "So I gather that you are dissatisfied. You feel cheated, because I did not reward you for your talents yesterday."

She seemed unsure of how to react. Nervously, she avoided his piercing black eyes. It had been easy enough to talk about him while he was out of the room, but now he was there, intimidating her with his presence. "I didn't mean what I said," she told him. "I mean about—about, you know, hurting you or anything like that. I mean, here we are, trapped, and it's only natural, you know, to build up a kind of resentment—"

"Of course," Josef agreed, enjoying her discomfort. I could tell he was playing a little game for his own purposes.

"It was her," Elizabeth went on, flashing me a poisonous look. "She got me saying things I didn't mean. She acts like she's better than the rest of us, like she's royalty or something. She bragged about all the things you gave her, and it didn't seem right. I mean, I could have done the things she did for you yesterday, all you had to do was ask me."

Elizabeth's voice trailed off into silence. She glanced at Josef, trying to gauge his response.

I couldn't restrain myself. "I've got to hand it to you," I said. "You really are quite an actress."

Elizabeth glared at me. She opened her mouth to reply. But Josef held up his hand, silencing us both. "Elizabeth—can you really do what Christina did?" he said. "Is that correct?"

Elizabeth hesitated. I was amused to see how willing she was to debase herself in front of the man she despised. That was her style: to sneer at men behind their backs, say how disgusting they were, and then grovel in front of them to win a few favors.

"You did say that," Josef persisted.

Elizabeth shrugged. "Of course. Of course I can do anything she can do. With the right man," she added, as if she thought she could give herself an easy out.

Josef laughed. He put his arm around Elizabeth and squeezed her up against him. With his other hand he caressed the side of her face, then let his fingers run down and follow the shape of her ample body. He nodded. "That's what I thought," he agreed. "You know, Elizabeth, perhaps you're right. Maybe I was not fair to you, and I was too generous to Christina." He smiled at Elizabeth, though his eyes were still sharp, as if they didn't see anything to smile at at all.

"After all," Josef went on, "you are certainly as beautiful as she is—or I would not have chosen you for my community."

I wondered what kind of game he was now playing. I was pretty damned sure he didn't find Elizabeth as attractive as me. Why else had he chosen me yesterday, so many times? Or had that been the game—to make me feel special, then deliberately undercut my ego and humiliate me? I tried not to show any of the resentment and uncertainty I was beginning to feel.

"Personally I have always found raven-haired women extremely exciting," Josef continued touching Elizabeth's hair. "I blame myself for not having given you a brush or a comb this morning. I'm sure you're right—that your . . . erotic talents . . . are every bit as intoxicating as Christina's." Then he glanced at me, as if he were mocking me. I felt sick inside, but I returned his glance, refusing to be embarrassed.

"The trouble is," Josef went on, "how can we ever know these things for sure? Perhaps, Elizabeth, you want to prove to me how irresistible you are. Then the matter will be settled once and for all.''

Now I saw what he'd been leading up to. She and I were going to have to compete to serve him. Which was fine—I knew I had a hell of a lot more to offer a man than that aging movie star, who obviously didn't even like men that much.

Josef walked away from us and opened the drapes, revealing the floor-to-ceiling mirrors, as he had the previous night. Then he took off his robe and reclined comfortably on some cushions. "Christina," he told me, "why don't you begin by coming here and making love to me where we can admire ourselves in the mirrors?"

"Of course," I said obediently. I walked across to him, ignoring the fact that everyone else in the room was watching me. "How may I please you?" I asked, kneeling down at his side, keeping myself strictly under control. At the back of my mind I wondered: Had he overheard a whispered conversation between myself and Alexandra? Did he suspect how I had planned to conquer him? Was this why he was humiliating me now? Or was he building up Elizabeth only to let her down even harder than before? I stared into Josef's eyes and tried to figure what he was doing, but it was impossible.

"Take off your leotard," he said, "and lie on top of me."

I started to obey him, but I took my time. I slipped first one arm out of the tight-fitting garment, then the other. Slowly, very slowly, I stretched the neck of it over my shoulders and started easing it down my body. I slipped my thumbs under the fabric and rolled it down, an inch at a time, over my breasts. The plump mounds of flesh came slowly into view. I revealed one nipple, then the other. I wriggled as I eased the leotard lower, and made my tits wobble and bounce. I saw

Josef watching them, and I saw his cock stiffen and lift its head. He reached down and began fondling himself while he continued watching me through half-closed eyes.

I finally rolled the leotard past my waist, and stood up and turned around as I slid it over my ass. The garment dropped to my ankles and I stepped out of it. Then, slowly, I turned around. I kept my hands at my sides and stood there for Josef's inspection, his willing servant, naked for his pleasure.

"Very nice," he agreed. "But I am still waiting for you to please me as I asked you to, Christina."

Now I was sure there was something wrong. He was rigging this event against me; I knew it. I could tell he'd enjoyed every second of watching me strip for him, and now he was just pretending to be impatient.

Well, I would try and beat him at his own game. I'd try and make it so fantastic for him, he would be unable to pretend that I couldn't please him properly.

I knelt astride him and lowered my body slowly onto him. I slipped my hands behind him and hugged myself to him, pressing my breasts against his chest. I stared into his eyes. Then, slowly and deliberately, I kissed him.

He barely responded. I could feel him holding himself in check. I moved my lips to his ear. "Why are you doing this to me?" I whispered. "Why are you humiliating me like this?"

He made no reply. A muscle twitched at the side of his face, revealing some inner tension, but I couldn't guess why.

He took me by the shoulders then, and turned me on my back. I lay on the cushions and looked up at him. His bearded face was inscrutable as he surveyed my body. He fingered his cock, which by this time was standing out straight and hard. Then, without any preliminaries, Josef lowered himself between my thighs, pushed the head of his cock between my labes, and thrust it into me.

I was barely aroused. If it hadn't been for my erotic dream about Gary, I would have been completely dry. I cried out as Josef pushed his cock up into me, fiercely and unfeelingly. He ignored me and started fucking me with quick, regular strokes.

I tried to recover my equilibrium. I reached up and caressed his face, then ran my hands through the hair on his chest. I fingered his nipples and, reaching lower, touched his cock as it slid in and out. I pulled my legs right up and rubbed my heels against his ass, urging him deeper into me, even though it still hurt a little. Then I clung to him, jerking my hips to meet each of his thrusts, and closed my mouth over his, kissing him long and deep.

I felt him beginning to respond, and I knew he was turned on by what I was doing. I only wished he had let me get on top, so that I could take control of the scene. I was sure, then, that I could have seduced him totally. But obviously that wasn't what he wanted.

He pulled away from me without warning, breaking my kiss and leaving me lying on my back like a fool, with my knees drawn up and my legs wide open. He rolled to one side, propped himself on an elbow, glanced at me dismissively and then looked across the room. "Your turn now, Elizabeth," he called to her.

I got up quickly, knowing that it would be futile to complain in any way. I grabbed my leotard and pulled it on in a few quick, angry movements. "I'm sorry you wouldn't let me please you more," I said, "unlike yesterday, when it seemed you couldn't get enough of me."

Josef raised his eyebrows. "Christina, you please me very much," he said. "Just as much as yesterday. But now it's Elizabeth's turn." Again the muscle twitched at the side of his face. He looked away from me to Elizabeth, and beckoned her toward him.

I went and sat down near Alexandra. I was feeling hurt that he had manipulated the whole thing. I had expected Josef to play fair somehow, but that was dumb of me—nothing he had done to us had been fair, in any sense. I remembered an article I once read about hostages who instinctively end up trying to please their captors in an attempt to win them over. I hoped that this syndrome wasn't happening to me. But I wasn't so sure anymore.

"You all right, Chris?" Alexandra whispered to me. "What the hell is going on?"

I shook my head. "I don't know—yet."

"Oh, well," she told me, "you know he's not to be trusted. You've just got to go on making yourself irresistible to him. You can get him in the end. I know it." She hugged me and kissed me on the cheek.

"I can't be irresistible if he makes up his mind to resist me," I objected.

Then I kept quiet. I wanted to watch exactly what happened with Elizabeth.

She walked over to Josef, wiggling her ass and sticking her tits out. She looked like a burlesque queen, I thought viciously. She looked cheap and old.

But Josef took it all in as if it really turned him on. "Take off your leotard," he told her. And he watched while she did a few more bumps and grinds, then shed the garment and tossed it aside. She put her hands on her hips and stood in a glamour-girl pose for his inspection.

"Very nice," he said, saying it exactly as he'd said it to me. "Now, Elizabeth. Show me how much you can please a man."

She got down on her knees between his legs and

started fondling his cock. She licked her lips and smiled at him coyly, but I could tell she wasn't really into it. She still hated his guts. But she was used to faking it with men, and she was determined to prove she could please him as much—or more—than me. Humiliating me would make it all worthwhile for her. That, and earning brownie points from Josef, so he'd give her the little luxuries she wanted.

She bent down and closed her lips around the head of his cock, then began moving her head up and down until a couple of inches were sliding in and out of her mouth. She put her hands behind his hips, and she worked harder on him. She took him deeper, then seemed to reach her limit—I saw she wasn't able to engulf the entire length of him as I had yesterday.

Josef must have realized this too. But he didn't want anyone else to see it. He reached down quickly and pulled her head up. "You will get astride me now," he told her.

She gave him her fake smile again and shook her tangled black hair out of her face. She edged up till her pussy was over his cock, then sat down on him. His cock was wet from where she'd sucked him, so it slid into her easily.

Elizabeth moved her knees up a little further, till she had the position right. Then she started fucking herself on Josef with short, rapid strokes. Her breasts wobbled and her flesh slapped against his. She started breathing hard. I could see she wasn't cut out for this kind of exertion. She was making the best of it, the short strokes costing her as little effort as possible, and the speed of her movements designed to make Josef come quickly. Even so, she was obviously getting tired.

Once again Josef intervened. He grabbed Elizabeth by her waist to stop her from moving. Then he rolled over, carrying her with him. He turned her on her back, braced himself, and started fucking her.

She lay under him passively, wriggling her body a little and giving girlish cries of excitement. She wrapped her legs around him, which, of course, just made it difficult for the poor guy to move in and out of her. She reared up and nipped at Josef's shoulder with her teeth, then at his ear, which, I was also sure, was absolutely the wrong kind of thing to do to a guy like him.

Josef increased the tempo of his thrusts, his hips jerking spasmodically. Suddenly he pulled out of her, reached down for his cock and held it as he came. The semen spurted out and splashed onto Elizabeth, onto her belly and her breasts. Josef moved up so that the very last drops fell upon her neck and face. He watched her all the while, and I sensed he was deliberately doing something he knew she'd find hard to take.

Elizabeth went on giving her little cries of fake excitement. She grimaced, though, and I was sure she didn't like the feel of the semen on her skin.

Josef rubbed the thick, white, creamy stuff into her breasts. "Good for the complexion, Elizabeth," he told her. Then he rubbed it across first one of her cheeks, then the other. "It'll make you even more beautiful," he told her.

Finally he got off her, found his discarded robe, and stood up, putting it on. He surveyed Elizabeth, then looked at me. He shrugged. "Christina, I have to admit I misjudged Elizabeth." He took her hand and helped her up onto her feet.

I said nothing, but I felt my face turn pink.

"In fact," Josef went on, "I don't like making comparisons, but—if I had to choose between the two of you—" He turned and pulled Elizabeth up against him, then closed one hand over her breast, put his other behind her neck, and kissed her long and hard.

CHAPTER SEVENTEEN

Elizabeth looked pleased with herself. After all, Josef had just told her the one thing she always wanted to hear: that she was more beautiful than anyone else. She fussed with her tangled hair for a moment, and ran her hands down over her body, admiring herself. Then she couldn't resist glancing in my direction with a smug little smile.

"Since you are so irresistible, Elizabeth," Josef said, placing his arm around her shoulders, "it seems to me that perhaps you are the woman who can help me with our Swiss friend, Michel." He paused thoughtfully and stroked his beard. "Come with me now, and help persuade him of his foolishness."

"What do you want me to do?" Elizabeth asked. She tried to sound willing, but I could see she was wondering exactly what Josef had in mind.

He started walking her to the door. "Oh, just a little visit with me to remind him of all the erotic fun that he's missing by staying in his room."

"You mean he has a choice, man?" Mark interrupted. He was sitting with his arm around Jane at one side of the room, from where he'd observed the events of the last half hour in silence. "We figured you'd locked the guy up," Mark went on.

Josef paused. "His door is locked, yes. But all of you have a choice, at any time, whether or not to cooperate. And those of you who cooperate are rewarded, as you already know.'' He turned to Elizabeth, grinned at her, and then kissed her on the cheek. It looked artificial to me, but she seemed to like it.

Josef turned back and faced the rest of us. ''If any of you are concerned about Michel—if you suspect he may be suffering in any way—why not come with me now to visit him?''

I stood up. ''Sure,'' I said. ''If you don't mind my company.''

''Christina, your company is always a pleasure.'' That sounded artificial too. I just couldn't figure him out.

''I'll join you,'' said Alexandra, standing up beside me.

''And you, Mark? And Jane?'' Josef asked, waiting expectantly.

''Forget it,'' the musician said, seeming to lose interest in the whole thing. ''I'm going to have another drink.''

''Very well,'' said Josef. ''Christina, Alexandra, come.''

We followed him out of the room and along the passageway. He reached in the pocket of his robe and pulled out his bunch of keys. I realized that if I'd thought of it, I could have filched those keys out of his pocket while his robe was on the floor when he was having sex with Elizabeth. And yet, thinking back, I remembered that although he'd dropped the robe casually, he'd left it close to where he lay. As usual, he had been careful and had taken all the right precautions.

He stopped outside the one cubicle door that was still locked, and then used a key to open it. He stood back to allow Elizabeth, Alexandra, and myself to enter the room ahead of him.

Michel was lying on his back on his bed, naked. At

first I thought he was taking it easy, stretched out calm and relaxed. Then I saw that he had no choice. Heavy leather straps had been locked around his wrists and ankles, and each strap was secured at a corner of the bed. In addition, a thick leather belt was tightly buckled around his waist, and that, too, was fastened to the bed. The most he could possibly do was move his head and squirm his body just a little.

"Good morning, Christina," Michel said, with a tight, humorless smile. "Alexandra. Elizabeth." His jaw clenched, and I could see he was mad as hell.

"Christ, how long have they had you tied down like this?" I asked him.

"They must have drugged me during the night and done it then," he said. "I woke up and my head ached. I tried to move my arms and legs, and that was when I found what had happened to me."

"You have only yourself to blame," said Josef, joining us in the tiny room.

Michel jerked in his bonds in a violent reflex as soon as he saw Josef. "Bastard!" he shouted. He tugged futilely at the straps, and I saw the leather dig into his skin. "When I get free—"

"When you get free, you won't have a single violent thought left in your head," Josef told him. "One way or another, my friend, we are determined to calm you down. In fact, Elizabeth here has come to help me persuade you how foolish you are to rebel against the pleasures I am offering you." Josef turned to Elizabeth. "Sit beside him on the bed and fondle him a little," he told her. "Yes, do it now, while we watch you."

Elizabeth forced an uneasy smile onto her face and reluctantly sat down beside Michel's immobilized naked body. She reached for his cock, which was lying limp amid curls of blond pubic hair.

Michel tried to jerk his hips away, but the strap

around his waist prevented him from moving more than an inch from side to side. "I do not want that whore to touch me!" he cried out. "Do not let her touch me!"

Elizabeth drew her hand back. She obviously didn't like having to deal with this.

But Josef merely smiled. "Ignore anything Michel says to you," he told Elizabeth. "He is not being rational. He knows perfectly well that you are a beautiful, irresistible woman. He knows that if you touch him, he will succumb to you. He cannot bear to have you undermine his willpower. So he insults you, to stop you from coming near him. Ignore his words and work your magic on him, my dear." He patted her on the shoulder. "The more quickly you can seduce him, the more pleased I will be. I will be very generous to you, Elizabeth." He gestured to Michel's crotch. "Go on, now. Fondle him."

Elizabeth obviously felt she had been given no choice. So she set her mind to the task. Once again she reached out for Michel's cock.

"No!" he shouted. "Goddamn you, I do not want that woman to—stop it!"

Elizabeth held his cock in her hand and started masturbating him.

"You are unclean," Michel shouted at her. "You—" He suddenly saw the futility of his insults, and tried one last time to twist free from his bonds. But the leather straps held him firmly. He groaned in despair, clamped his eyes shut, and turned his face toward the wall.

Josef patted Elizabeth on the shoulder. "You see, he soon understood how hopeless it is to try to resist. Use your mouth on him."

She glanced up at him plaintively, as if to say, 'Do I have to?' But she could see in his face the inevitable answer.

I had been watching Josef carefully myself. As usual, he was trying not to show any trace of emotion. But I was learning how to read him, and I was convinced he was getting a big kick out of having Michel in bondage with Elizabeth forced to serve him. He looked toward me suddenly and caught me watching his face. And then, to my amazement, he winked at me.

It happened in just an instant, and then he was once again stony-faced, fearsome, and solemn. I almost thought his winking at me must have been my imagination. And yet I knew it wasn't. So he did have a special kind of a feeling for me, after all. At least, that seemed to be what he had conveyed just then, or was even this part of his game? I realized I could go crazy trying to interpret his actions.

Meanwhile, Elizabeth was working hard at sucking Michel's cock. She had stretched out between Michel's legs and was supporting herself on her elbows on either side of his hips, her head bobbing up and down. Her thick black hair concealed her face, so we couldn't tell exactly what was happening. But I noted that Michel's body was tense, the muscles showing clearly under his tanned skin. I knew very well that the first step to turning a man on was to persuade him to relax, so it looked to me as if Elizabeth wasn't going to have too much success with him.

Sure enough, after a minute more she gave up. She rolled off Michel and looked up at Josef hopelessly. "He won't let himself respond to me," she said, gesturing at Michel's penis, which was still lying limp, no larger than it had been when she started.

Josef shrugged. "I knew he would not be easy," he said. "That is why I need a beautiful woman to persuade him. Try some more, Elizabeth. I'm sure you will succeed."

"But—" Her voice rose to a whine. "I can't! Why not

get Christina to do it? She did it with him yesterday, didn't she? I mean she gets off on giving men head. She told me she can't get enough of it.''

I opened my mouth to argue, but Josef gestured for me to be quiet. ''You seem to forget,'' he told Elizabeth, ''that we just proved to everyone's satisfaction that you are much more irresistible than Christina. Is that not true?''

Elizabeth stared petulantly at the floor and said nothing.

''Get back on the bed,'' Josef ordered her. His voice was suddenly harsh and commanding. ''And do what I tell you. Otherwise I will be very disappointed in you, Elizabeth. I will have to take back all that I have offered you.''

She looked sick, but she did what he said. While Michel lay there, still with his eyes tightly shut and his face turned away from us all, Elizabeth took his cock and resumed licking and sucking it.

''Very good,'' said Josef, patting her on the head. He glanced at Alexandra, standing beside me, watching the display. ''You stay here, Alexandra, and make sure that Elizabeth does all she can to arouse this man. And call us at once if she has any success. We must persuade him, even if it takes a couple of hours. Understand?''

Alexandra nodded. I could see she was as pleased as I was to see Elizabeth in the role of servant.

''Do you want me to help Elizabeth out at all?''

Josef shook his head. ''No. She is such a formidable woman, she will need no help.'' A flicker of a smile showed on his face.

He turned to me and took my arm. ''Christina, we will go back to the main room.'' Then he led me back out into the hallway. I glanced behind me for one last look at Elizabeth, who raised her head from Michel's crotch and flashed me a look of pure hatred.

Josef closed the door of the room behind us but

didn't lock it. We started walking along the hallway toward the orgy room, and I debated with myself whether to say anything to him about the games he'd been playing. Suddenly he stopped me and pushed my back against the wall of the corridor.

He held me by the shoulders and looked down into my eyes. "Christina," he said slowly, thoughtfully. And then he kissed me hard. Suddenly he was passionate, revealing all the erotic feeling that he'd held back from me earlier. The weight of his body trapped me against the wall, and soon his hands moved down and grabbed my breasts while his mouth pressed insistently on mine. I felt overwhelmed by him.

His cock stirred and rose up against my thighs. I reached down and started fondling it, and within a minute it was fully erect and pushing insistently against my crotch.

Josef broke our kiss for a moment. He stroked his fingers down my cheek. "Christina," he said again, as if savoring the word. "I have been wanting this."

"You were offered it earlier," I said, speaking without thinking. As soon as the words were out of my lips, I realized I might have seemed rebellious. Luckily he didn't get angry.

"Earlier, I could not accept your offer," he said. And I thought there was actually a troubled look in his eyes. "Do not ask questions," he added firmly. "Just accept that I could not enjoy you then. But I can, now. Quickly, right here. Please me, Christina—with your mouth." He kissed me again. "Do that for me."

He was so intense, so focused on me, it was scary. Still, I knew how to give him what he wanted, and it was good to have my suspicions confirmed—that he really did have a special interest in me.

I dropped to my knees and took his cock between my lips. He was obviously so worked up, I didn't try to take it slowly or tantalize him. I swallowed him deep, deep into my mouth and throat. Then I began moving my head as quickly as I could. His stiff, thick flesh slid in and out across my tongue. I sucked him hard and felt his cock strain and stiffen.

But even this wasn't enough to satisfy his impatience. He suddenly seized my head between his hands, forced me back against the wall, then held me there and started moving his hips in urgent, sudden jerks.

I gave myself up to it, becoming totally passive, accepting his cock as he thrust it deep into my mouth. I even felt a kind of romantic passion in all of it, letting the man have total use of my body. He was proving how much he needed and wanted me compared with anyone else available to him. Every thrust, every gasp told me that. It excited me, and I felt pleased with myself for being able to have such an effect on him. I was now sure he would soon be sexually addicted to me.

His hips moved faster and faster, and his hands clenched where he held my head. He groaned and then shouted with pleasure as the erotic sensations overwhelmed him. He came, and I tasted his jism and drank the essence of him. I wrapped my arms behind his ass and held his cock deep, till the spasms ended and I had consumed every last drop of his come.

Then I released him and he pulled back from me. He was gasping for breath and seemed a little weak at the knees. He reached down and helped me stand up beside him, then kissed me hard. He didn't seem to mind the taste of his own come on my lips and tongue.

"Christina," he murmured, holding me tight against his chest. "I needed that—needed to feel—" He broke off in mid-sentence, perhaps realizing he was revealing a little too much of his desires for me.

I kissed him on the cheek. "My pleasure," I whispered.

He ran his hand down my nakedness. He started to say something more, but at that moment a sudden noise interrupted him. We both turned our heads in surprise as we heard, from the direction of the orgy room, the crash of breaking glass.

CHAPTER EIGHTEEN

Josef ran down the hallway, and I ran after him. We went through the door into the communal orgy room, and both of us stopped dead.

The big floor-to-ceiling mirror that covered one wall of the room had been smashed. Giant pieces of glass were strewn across the carpet and the cushions where Elizabeth and I had had sex with Josef just a little earlier.

Jane was huddled in a far corner of the room, looking terrified. Mark was nowhere to be seen. And then, as I looked at the big hole in the mirror, I realized—there was no wall behind it. There was, in fact another room beyond it.

Suddenly I understood: It was a one-way mirror, through which Carl and Helen Stanowski must have watched all of us while we played our sex games with Josef. That was why Josef had always insisted on doing everything near the glass: so that the Stanowskis could have a grandstand view.

And now, somehow, Mark had smashed the mirror, and had escaped through the hole he had made. At least, that was the way it looked.

Evidently, Josef reached the same conclusion. He started to run forward, but then hesitated. There was glass all over the floor, and he had no shoes on at that moment. If he went after Mark he'd cut himself to pieces.

He turned around to me. "Stay in here," he said curtly, then ran out of the room, back along the corridor. I heard him unlock the main exit door and dash upstairs. The door slammed shut behind him, so I was still trapped down in the basement—unless I chose to try to make it out through the broken mirror myself.

I turned to Jane. "What happened?" I asked her.

"He said he couldn't take it anymore," she said, wide-eyed and afraid. "He tore some pillows apart and wrapped the cloth around his hands and feet, then he went for the mirror. I guess he'd figured out there was another room behind it."

I nodded. Smart guy—at least he was smarter than he seemed. Except, of course, he was probably still trapped in the building, and worse, still hooked on the drug like all of us.

Unless—maybe—there were some supplies of it lying around upstairs, and Josef's story about it all being kept in a locked safe was just a story.

I figured there was only one way to find out. I grabbed a pillow and did what Jane said Mark had done: I tore it open and wrapped cloth around my feet. Then I found my own discarded leotard lying on the floor, shook fragments of glass out of it, and put it on quickly.

I paused to listen, but there wasn't a sound; obviously Alexandra and Elizabeth were still with Michel, unaware that anything had happened. The cubicles were so well soundproofed that they wouldn't have heard anything. And presumably Robert French was still in his cubicle too.

I turned to Jane. "I'm going exploring," I told her. "In the meantime, find a piece of the glass that's long and sharp. Like a dagger, get it? Then hide it somewhere, but not in your room. Maybe find a way to slip it under the carpet in here. All right?"

She nodded dumbly. I didn't know whether she'd really do what I'd told her, but it was worth a try. Any kind of weapon could be useful to us in days to come.

I turned and crunched across the broken glass toward the smashed mirror. Mark had done a thorough job— the gaping hole was five feet high and a couple of feet wide. I picked my way though it.

On the other side of the glass I found the Stanowski's little paradise of voyeurism. There was a big bed with pillows piled on it, a couple of pairs of binoculars, a video camera, a video recorder, and a stack of cassettes. On one wall was a video projection screen. I could imagine them cuddling up together on the bed, treating themselves to a display of our sex games visible through the giant mirror. Then later they could replay the whole thing from their tapes.

I turned and looked back through what was left of the mirror. The silvered glass had the effect of dimming the lights of the orgy room slightly. But generally speaking, visibility was still excellent. My flesh crawled, however, at the thought of having been ogled by that creepy little guy and his sister.

I turned and went across the plushly furnished video room to a door standing open beside the big bed, then peeked through and found a stairway leading up to the floor above. I listened: There were faint sounds, but I couldn't figure what they were.

I started up the stairs, my heart thudding almost painfully. I knew if Josef found me he would be angry as hell, and he'd realize I was more rebellious than I'd seemed to be. Here I was, directly disobeying him, going where I knew I shouldn't go.

But I had to see if there was any opportunity for escape.

The stairs were newly installed, and they didn't creak, thank God. The walls were of concrete, painted white, and there was a single light on the ceiling at the top of the landing. I walked up and found another open door at the top leading into the upper part of the building.

Once again, I paused and listened. I could hear voices, but they were some way off.

I poked my head out the door and took a quick look. There was a corridor which seemed to run the whole length of the building, its floor covered with thick red carpet. There was a grotesquely pretentious chandelier hanging from the ceiling halfway down the hall, and the walls throughout the corridor were done in red velvet wallpaper. The place looked like a brothel. I hadn't realized Josef had such bad taste.

Some of the doors along the passageway were standing half open. The distant voices that I could hear seemed to be coming from a door at the end of the passage. Slowly, softly, I started out of my hiding place and crept along, my cloth-wrapped feet silent on the thick carpet.

I came to the first door that stood half open. I hesitated. My throat was dry and my heart was still pounding. Cautiously, I listened at the door, then peeped through it.

It was a bedroom. Was it Josef's? The decor was intimidating—all the walls were painted flat black, with moldings of gold and silver. There were big paintings of erotic art, a Jacuzzi in one corner, and a huge bed covered in animal skins. There was, of course, no window. Only spotlights played upon a pure white carpet.

The place was empty. I walked in slowly, thinking I might be able to find out who occupied this room.

There was a giant antique bureau standing against the wall behind the door. I started going through the drawers. First I found only clothes—everything either black or white, and most of the garments made of silk. I tried to leave everything looking as I found it, but my hands were shaking and I was in too much of a hurry to do the job neatly.

Finally, in the bottom drawer, I came upon something interesting. Here was the book of pictures Josef had first shown me, "introducing" me to my fellow members of his commune. And there was also a notebook in a black leather cover. I opened it eagerly—and found a brief record of each person's date of abduction and arrival at the house by the ocean where we had first been taken. The only names, though, were those of myself and my fellow prisoners.

I rummaged around some more and found a wallet, which I also opened quickly. In it were credit cards and a driver's license, but I realized that the picture on the license was of Robert French. As I looked further, I found personal possessions of all of the prisoners. It was clear that Helen Stanowski had lied to me; my jewelry and other effects had not, in fact, been destroyed.

I opened a jewelry box that I found at the back of the drawer, and sure enough, among the items that belonged to Jane, Alexandra, and Elizabeth, I found my own necklace, rings, and earrings.

I wished I could keep them, but I didn't want to leave any sign of my having been in the room. So I replaced everything carefully and closed the drawer.

Suddenly, from the room at the far end of the corridor, I heard voices louder than before. And then a shout—it sounded like Mark, in pain. Christ, I thought, what were they doing to him?

I slipped out of what I thought was Josef's bedroom and sidled a little farther along the corridor. Surely Josef would go back downstairs any minute to check that I was obeying instructions—or did he think I wouldn't be so crazy as to try and follow Mark upstairs?

I heard another shout from the room at the end of the corridor. This time I was sure it was Mark's voice. I had to see what was happening, so I ran to the last door and peeked through the crack between it and its frame.

I saw a large room full of weird pieces of equipment, a room that seemed like a cross between a laboratory and a kinky-sex club. There was a bench with glassware and a microscope, shelves of reference books, and other kinds of laboratory equipment that I couldn't recognize: tubes and steel boxes and something that looked like a computer.

In the center of the room stood a big padded table, like a massage table. But this one had spotlights shining down on it, video equipment set up beside it—and Mark who was strapped onto the table, facedown, bare-ass naked.

His wrists and ankles were secured just as Michel's had been downstairs. I glimpsed Carl and his sister in their white lab coats. She was holding a 35-mm camera while he peered through a video camera. And as I shifted position, still peeking through the crack at the hinge end of the door, I saw Josef standing holding a riding crop.

"Show Mr. Bernstein once again how much we disapprove of his destructive behavior," Helen Stanowski said to Josef. "Make it clear to him, please."

Helen giving orders to Josef? That didn't make sense—but Josef did what she told him. He raised the riding crop and brought it down hard across Mark's naked behind.

Mark twisted and yelled, and the crop left a bright red mark. I counted five or six other marks that had already been inflicted—neat, parallel welts across the cheeks of his ass.

Josef flexed his shoulders under his embroidered black robe, raised the crop, and brought it down again. I heard the *thwack* of it and saw Mark's flesh jump and quiver. I remember how Josef had spanked Jane, and how he'd seemed to enjoy every moment of it, but now he wasn't showing the same kind of pleasure.

"Very nice," I heard Helen Stanowski say as the shutter of her camera clicked. I didn't like her tone of voice; she sounded as if she became aroused by seeing Mark punished.

"We must not forget about the rest of them," said Carl. "Josef, secure the basement before we proceed up here.

Josef nodded. "Right away."

"For fuck's sake, let me out of this thing, man!" Mark shouted, twisting and tugging at the restraints. "So I broke your goddamned mirror. So what? What do you expect? You treat us like animals, man. What do you expect us to do?"

Helen Stanowski stepped forward. She slapped Mark's face with one neat, precise movement of her hand. "Quiet," she told him. "You will learn to obey."

"Fuck you!" Mark shouted at her, and I had to admire his insolence, though under the circumstances, it seemed dumb.

"Josef!" said Helen. "Punish him again!"

But Carl intervened. "We really must secure the basement first," he told her. Reluctantly she agreed.

Josef put down the riding crop and stepped toward the door where I was hiding.

Immediately I turned and ran, taking great leaping strides. Because my feet were still wrapped in the pieces of torn cloth, Josef couldn't hear me running. I figured I could just about make it to the stairway, but then, only a few paces away from it, one of the bits of cloth unwrapped itself and tripped me.

I fell hard onto my knees and elbows, and sprawled full-length on the red carpet. I bit my lip to stop myself from crying out in pain, but my body hurt like hell. Nonetheless I scrambled up quickly—although not quickly enough. I glanced behind me and saw Josef emerge from the room at the end of the corridor.

I started toward the stairway, hoping I might still make it, but that was a forlorn hope. Just as I reached the exit he looked in my direction and I froze, feeling an awful sinking sensation inside.

It was all over. He had seen me.

CHAPTER NINETEEN

I knew there was no point in running away from him; there was nowhere to run. So I stood there, helpless and trapped as he walked down the corridor toward me.

He stopped a couple of steps away. I was about to speak—to give him some feeble excuse for being there—but he quickly brought his finger to my lips, urging me to be silent.

Then he took my arm and motioned me to accompany him back along the corridor. I resisted, fearing he intended to drag me into the same room where I'd seen Mark strapped to the padded table, but Josef quickly understood what I was thinking. He patted me gently on the arm as if to reassure me, and pointed to a different door near the end of the passageway.

Reluctantly, I went with him. He walked slowly, and I saw that his eyes were alert and wary. I couldn't figure exactly what he was up to, but obviously he didn't want the Stanowskis to see that he had me with him. Which was just fine, as far as I was concerned.

Slowly, silently, he opened the door he had pointed to, which was only a few feet from the door into Carl's laboratory, or whatever the room was where they held Mark. I could hear the murmur of the Stanowskis' voices, with an occasional angry complaint from Mark. Well, I thought, at least he's not being punished anymore—for the time being.

Then Josef directed me through the door he had selected, and I found myself in the small, bare, wood-paneled room we had first been herded into when we were taken off the truck. From this room the main staircase led down to the basement.

Josef directed me ahead of him, and I went quickly down the stairs. I reached the main door into the basement and found that there was a handle that opened it from the outside without the need of a key. Josef followed me, and the door closed itself behind us.

I felt relieved to be back down in the basement near our row of cubicles, although of course I knew I was no safer down there than I was anywhere else.

I looked up at Josef questioningly. "What—" I began.

He bent his head to mine and whispered directly into my ear. "I can tell you nothing now. Be patient. Most of all remember: No matter what I may say later—no matter what anyone says—you did not, you absolutely did not, go upstairs." And then he straightened up and said loudly, "Christina, fetch Alexandra and Elizabeth. And Mr. French, also. Bring them to me in the main room. We have a lot of clearing up to do, thanks to Mark Bernstein's act of wanton destruction." Then, without waiting for my response, he turned and walked briskly away to the room at the end of the hall.

I wanted to go after him and ask what he'd meant, but I had the distinct impression he was afraid of our conversation being overheard by the Stanowskis via the surveillance system. I started wondering exactly what his relationship was with them—I'd always assumed he was in total command. I wanted to start asking questions, but I decided I would have to be patient. So I went in to Michel's cubicle.

Alexandra and Elizabeth were still in there. I realized it had been only about fifteen minutes since I had been in there myself with Josef.

They obviously had no idea that anything had happened. Elizabeth was lying stretched out on top of Michel, wearily rubbing her tits to and fro across his chest and trying to kiss him on the mouth. He turned his head away, though, avoiding her every time. I could see that despite her best efforts to arouse him, his cock was still limp in her grip.

"Don't give up yet, Elizabeth," Alexandra was saying. "You know what Josef said—even if it takes a couple of hours . . ." Then she looked up at me. "What's going on, Chris?"

"Quite a lot," I said. "Mark flipped out and tried to escape. Managed to break the big mirror in the orgy room, but the mirror was a false front, concealing another room behind it. Mark got through the hole in the glass and went up some back stairs, from the concealed room to the floor above. But they caught him and—" I broke off, realizing that if Josef wanted me to pretend I hadn't been upstairs myself, I shouldn't be able to know that Mark had been caught.

. "At least," I went on, "I assume they caught Mark. Anyway, we're wanted in the orgy room to sweep up the mess."

"Jesus Christ," Alexandra muttered. She turned to Elizabeth. "You hear all that? We'd better go in there right away."

"Thank God," she exclaimed, pulling herself up off Michel. "I won't forget all this, you little whore," she said, glowering at me. "I know you set me up with Josef, to get me to do this to Michel. Don't try to deny it. All you wanted was to see me publicly humiliated."

"Isn't that what you wanted for me?" I countered.

Alexandra stepped between us. "Later, all right?" she said, looking from one of us to the other.

Reluctantly, Elizabeth turned away. She assembled

what was left of her dignity and strode out of the cubicle without another glance in my direction.

"Christina," Michel called to me from his position on the bed. "What *did* happen to Mark? Is it bad?"

"I tell you, I have no way of knowing."

He looked at me skeptically. "There is something you are not saying," he said. "I wonder now how much any of us should trust each other. I still do not forgive you, Christina, for what you did to me yesterday evening."

I thought back and realized he was talking about my having seduced him. I shrugged. "Well, looks like you're protecting your virtue pretty successfully today," I said, "despite Elizabeth's best efforts."

"I do not see this as a joke," he murmured. I noticed the tension in his body and realized he must have felt that he had lost all his dignity.

"Any chance we can get him loose from those straps?" I asked Alexandra, feeling sorry for him.

"No the straps are fastened with padlocks. And there's nothing we've been given that could cut leather. After Josef left I tried using my teeth, but it was hopeless."

Privately I thought of the shard of glass that I'd told Jane to hide. But I didn't even know if she'd done what I'd told her. "All right," I said, "let's go meet Josef and see what he wants."

Alexandra caught my arm. "Chris—wait. I still haven't had a chance to tell you what happened to me last night."

I hesitated. "Yeah, you mentioned something—but you know, they could be listening in on us right now."

She shook her head. "I'm only telling you what they already know. Carl Stanowski came to visit me. I woke up and found him in my room."

I frowned. "He did? I told him you were interested in him. Did he make any advances?"

"No. That was the weird part about it. He came in with his sister. She told me not to move a muscle, and she stood right by the bed. She had a hypodermic in her hand, and I know these people don't kid around with their drugs, so I did exactly what they told me. And then Carl . . . measured me."

I laughed. "He what?"

"I tell you, the little guy measured me. He had a measuring tape, and he measured my arms, my legs, every damn part of me—the distance between my nipples and my crotch, etc. He read out each measurement—into a tape recorder, I guess—and then he and his sister walked out and left me alone again." She put her hands on her hips. "What do you make of that?"

"This is all getting to be too much to deal with," I said. I wished I could tell her about my adventure upstairs—but clearly Josef wanted nothing said out loud about that, and anyway Michel was here listening to us. I wasn't prepared to confide in anyone other than Alexandra.

"At first," she said, "when Carl pulled out that tape, I thought, oh shit, he's measuring me for a coffin."

I patted her reassuringly. "Maybe he gets off on vital statistics," I told her. "Look, we can drive ourselves crazy trying to guess what it all means. He could just have done something deliberately freaky to make you worry about it. It could mean nothing at all."

"Maybe," she agreed doubtfully.

"Look, we better get back to the orgy room," I told her, then took a last look at Michel. "Sorry we can't do anything for you, Michel. I'll bring you some breakfast, if they let me."

But he turned his head away and refused to answer.

Alexandra and I walked over to Robert French's cubicle. He seemed to be in the same state as before:

spaced-out. I was sure they had him on some kind of heavy tranquilizer. He looked like someone who had been lobotomized.

"You have to come with us to the communal room, Robert," I told him.

He looked at me with a puzzled expression. "Where?"

"Just come with us," said Alexandra, and guided him out of his cubicle and along the corridor.

In the main room I found Josef supervising everyone while Elizabeth and Jane picked up the biggest pieces of broken glass, using scraps of cloth to protect their hands. Josef saw me walk in with Alexandra and French. He seized my arm angrily. "Where have you been?" he demanded.

I flinched from the loudness of his voice. He changed so quickly, I couldn't tell if he was acting or if this was for real. I decided it was probably an act—but in Josef there was a fine line between role-playing and the real thing. For the moment I knew I'd better take him seriously.

"Alexandra and I stayed a moment to talk to Michel," I said meekly. "He's hungry, and—"

"He'll be a lot hungrier before I allow him any food," Josef said. Suddenly he walked over to me, grabbed me roughly by the shoulders, and forced me to look into his face. "Jane tells me that you tried to follow Mark Bernstein through the hole in the mirror. Is that true?"

I winced from the pain of Josef's grip. He was playing this altogether too realistically—so much so, he made me want to confess what had really happened. But I remembered what he'd whispered to me earlier. "I did go through the hole in the mirror," I admitted. "Ouch, that hurts!"

"I ordered you to stay in this room, didn't I?" he

demanded, clenching my shoulders even tighter than before.

I felt tears starting at the corners of my eyes. "Yes," I agreed.

"Yes, what?" he demanded.

"Yes, master."

"So? What did you do after you went through to the room beyond the mirror?"

I thought quickly. His act was convincing, but I knew, I just knew he wanted me to lie. "I came straight back into the room here," I told him. "Then I went to find Alexandra and Elizabeth, which is where you found me, just outside Michel's cubicle." I gasped. "Please! You're hurting me!"

Actually, it didn't hurt that much. But if he was going to do some acting, why not me, too?

Slowly, Josef released his grip. "Why did you go through into the room beyond the mirror?" he asked me. "Why did you disobey my orders?"

"I—just wanted to see what was in there," I told him. "I didn't think it would matter, just to have a look."

He grunted. "It matters that you disobeyed me. You will be punished. Now get to work with the others. Pick up this mess and stack all the glass in the corner there. I will go and get something for you to put the pieces in." Then, without another word, he strode out of the room. I heard him open the main exit, which then slammed shut behind him. Well, I thought, I hope I played my part the way he wanted me to.

"Gee, honey, you sure got on the wrong side of him," said Elizabeth, with a smirk. "Hope he doesn't hit you too hard when it's time for you to get what's coming to you."

I tried to ignore her and started helping to gather up the broken glass.

"So, what's behind the mirror?" Alexandra asked me. "What did you find?"

"I only had a quick look," I told her—I was being truthful, in a way. "I think it's the Stanowskis' love nest. There's a big bed and a video camera. I think they're heavily into voyeurism. They must have watched us having sex in here, through the mirror."

Alexandra laughed. "That figures. But there must be a separate entrance to the little room back there. Is that the way to the back stairs up to the ground floor?" She picked her way carefully to the hole in the mirror and peered through.

"Josef went in there already," said Jane. "I heard him shut a door and lock it. Than he came back out."

So the basement had been secured, I thought to myself, in accordance with Helen Stanowski's instructions.

"I'm sorry, Chris," Jane went on. "I guess I shouldn't have told Josef you went in there. But—that's all I said, you know, nothing more than that." She looked at me hard. I nodded as if to tell her that I understood her implication—that she hadn't said anything about my going upstairs. Had Josef warned her, too, to forget that such a thing had happened? Either way, she must be now wondering how I'd disappeared up the back stairs and come in again the front way. There was no way to reconcile all the different stories; I felt myself growing more an more tangled in a web of contradictions that could never be explained.

As I helped the others gather up the pieces of the broken mirror, only one question now seemed important: Who was really in charge here? Josef—or Helen Stanowski?

CHAPTER TWENTY

We worked for a while, clearing up the mess. I considered trying to hide a piece of the glass myself in case Jane hadn't done so, but I had the uneasy feeling that, because I had defied Josef, we might very well be under surveillance now. For the same reason I didn't want to risk asking Jane whether she'd done what I suggested.

Josef returned with some garbage bags and we completed the cleanup. He had gone through another mood change and now seemed distant and unreachable, unfriendly toward me and everyone else. As soon as the glass was all swept up and bagged, he told us to go into our cubicles. He locked us in, one by one, saying that there'd be a meeting of the whole group in the communal room later that afternoon. When he left me in my cubicle he avoided looking at me and said nothing.

I washed up and lay down on my bed. I tried to reconstruct the events of the last few hours, once again trying to figure out what everything meant. But there was no way I could integrate it into a single picture that made any sense.

I wondered if Mark Bernstein was all right—I hoped they weren't mistreating him. But as usual there was absolutely nothing I could do except wait. My best hope, as before, lay in trying to seduce Josef so that he would find me irresistible, which would give me greater control over him.

Unfortunately, though, time passed very slowly. Hours later, Josef came back, unlocked my door, and told me to go into the communal room.

When I got there I found Elizabeth, Alexandra, Jane, Robert French, and Helen and Carl Stanowski all sitting on cushions in a semicircle. There was an uneasy silence. Josef followed me into the room, closed the door, and then directed me to join the others. I felt as if some kind of pronouncement or lecture was going to be given—it was an ominous sensation, perhaps because Josef himself looked so grim. Everyone was looking at me, as though they knew something I didn't know, and it wasn't going to be good news.

I sat down with the others. Josef stood in the center of the group, surveying us all for a long moment. Behind him, I saw that the drapes had been pulled across the shattered mirror to hide it from view. The room once again looked clean and comfortable, deceptively civilized.

"I have been very disappointed with the behavior of the male members of our community," Josef said. He measured each word and stared slowly at each of us in turn. "First, Mr. French here decided to—run away." He said it with a look of disgust. "Well, you can see how we have rehabilitated Mr. French."

I looked at Robert. He still had the same dazed, blank expression as before. It was creepy.

"Next, our Swiss friend decided to refuse to participate in any of our entertainments," Josef went on. "No sooner had we isolated him in his cubicle—where he remains at this moment—than our musician, Mr. Bernstein, decided to take matters into his own hands."

Josef turned, stepped to the drapes, and pulled one of them aside for a moment to reveal the hole in the mirror. Then he walked back to us. "Mr. Bernstein is now being given time to consider the error of his ways.

Such actions are stupid because, as you well know, they cannot achieve anything. I am in complete control here. If you wish to survive in comfort, you will obey me."

Privately, I wondered again how true his statement was about being in sole command. Certainly from Josef's manner no one could have imagined that he was not the ruler of his domain. And yet . . .

"I am now concerned," he went on, "that some of our female members might be tempted to follow the bad example of the men. There has already been one hint of this." He suddenly turned and pointed at me. "You, Christina, directly disobeyed my order to stay in this room. You followed Mark Bernstein into the anteroom beyond the mirror." He glowered at me. "It's fortunate for you that you went no farther. Otherwise, you would be enjoying the same rehabilitative therapy that Mr. Bernstein is currently experiencing. "Luckily for you, your disobedience is minor, but it must be dealt with, nonetheless, to make it clear that I will not tolerate rebelliousness."

I felt a chill in my stomach. What did he have in store for me? Although he seemed to be protecting me by still pretending that I had never strayed out of the basement, I could sense he was going to make an example out of me, and it wouldn't be pleasant.

He walked over to where I was sitting meekly on my cushion on the floor. "Do you have anything to say for yourself, Christina?" He reached down, grabbed me by the hair and jerked my head back so that I was looking up at him.

"I didn't mean to disobey you." I lied. "It was thoughtlessness, not rebelliousness."

He grunted. "We will help you think a little more carefully next time." He let go of me and turned to the Stanowskis. "Carl! Fetch me the crop."

His voice was loud and commanding. Carl got to his

feet immediately, went across the room, and came back with a riding crop that looked like the one I had seen Josef use on Mark upstairs. Oh Christ, I thought—I don't want that thing raising welts on my ass.

"Give the crop to Elizabeth," Josef told Carl. The little guy nodded obediently and put the riding crop in Elizabeth's hands. She looked at him, then at me, and her look of puzzlement gradually turned to one of understanding, and then anticipation. I saw the maliciousness in her eyes and I felt sick.

"Helen," Josef said, turning to Helen Stanowski. "Turn up the lights so that we can see every detail of Christina van Bell's humiliation."

Obediently Helen got to her feet and went to the light switch and dimmer control by the door.

You bastard, I thought to myself, staring resentfully at Josef. Each time I figured I could trust him, he turned on me. He could have made some show of punishing me without taking it this far—without getting Elizabeth to give me my comeuppance. He knew how she disliked me.

"Christina!" Josef yelled, interrupting my thoughts. "Come here!" He stood with his arms folded and waited for me to scramble up and go to him. I stopped in front of him, my arms by my sides, then looked up at him, thinking perhaps the sight of me looking sad and submissive might soften him a bit.

But his stern expression never changed. He reached in the pocket of his robe and brought out a couple of lengths of red velvet rope. "Bend down and touch your toes, Christina," he told me.

I knew there was no point in refusing—it would only intensify my eventual punishment. So I did as I was bid.

"Carl! Helen!" Josef called. "You know what to do."

I'd never heard him command them in such a lordly manner. Did he feel his authority had been undermined by Mark's act of rebellion? Or was he trying to prove some other point?

I felt the presence of Carl and Helen Stanowski on either side of me, then felt their fingers on my wrists, tying the rope there. While I stood doubled over, they knelt and tied the other end of each rope to my ankles, so that each wrist was secured to each ankle. Naturally, I was unable to straighten up. I had to stand there with my ass in the air.

I knew what was going to happen next. Sure enough, I heard Josef shout, "Elizabeth! Come here. Helen, Carl—hold Christina steady."

I felt their hands on my body, but in my bent-over position my face was at the level of my knees, and my vision was mostly blocked off by my hair hanging down. I bit my lip, determined not to give anyone the satisfaction of hearing me cry out.

Then I felt Josef's hand undoing my leotard at the crotch. He peeled the garment up, exposing my bottom. His hands were steady and firm in their movements as he stroked his fingers across my skin, almost soothingly, as if to reassure me. But that could have just been my fantasy, because I sure as hell didn't feel any more friendly toward him for his little gesture of kindness, if that's what it was. Right then I hated the bastard.

"You will use the riding crop on Christina," Josef told Elizabeth. "Ten strokes across her bottom."

I closed my eyes and waited, but the waiting was the worst part—anticipating how that bad-tempered bitch would do her worst, while everyone else watched my humiliation.

Then I felt the first blow, a sudden smack across my ass, followed by a quick wave of burning sensations that stung me and made me wince and grit my teeth.

Still, it wasn't half as bad as I had feared—luckily, Elizabeth was in pretty bad shape; she didn't have the strength to hit me really hard.

"Shall I do it again?" I heard her say with pleasure.

"Yes, nine more strokes," said Josef. "As fast or as slowly as you wish."

The second blow fell, and the third came quickly after it. Those lashes didn't add a lot to the overall discomfort, but my whole ass started to throb with a kind of glowing pain. Instinctively I tried to pull away, but the Stanowskis kept a firm grip on me.

There was a long pause before the fourth stroke from the riding crop. Elizabeth was deliberately maintaining the suspense. "Does it hurt, honey?" I heard her ask. Then I felt her hand on my ass, and so help me, she pinched me. I felt a great surge of anger and disgust— but I still kept my mouth shut and said nothing.

My silence must have annoyed her, because she started hitting me again. She counted out each blow, from four through ten, but I shut my eyes and endured it. Then I felt the Stanowskis undoing the rope at my ankles and wrists.

I straightened up as soon as they released me. Josef grabbed me by the shoulders. "You will repeat after me, Christina: 'I will never disobey you again.' "

I took a shaky breath, not knowing whether to be angry or hurt. The skin of my ass was stinging; I could feel the lines where the riding crop had struck; and I was too embarrassed to face the others, who had watched me being beaten. At the same time, I wanted to do something really bad to Josef—knee him in the balls, hit him in the face, anything.

But I reined in my rebelliousness. "I will never disobey you again," I said, though the words almost choked me.

"Master," he added.

"I will never disobey you again, master," I told him.

"Now kiss my feet," he ordered me.

Jesus Christ, I thought to myself, how much more of this would I have to take? But I got down on my knees and kissed his bare feet. Then I stood up again, still facing him, not wanting to turn around and look at the rest of the group—Elizabeth least of all.

"Very good, Christina," said Josef, his voice suddenly soft and mellow. He gave my shoulder a pat. "Now go to your cubicle."

I think he knew that I couldn't look anyone in the eye, and he wanted to spare me that. Maybe there was some sort of decency in him after all. I didn't know. I reached behind me, rolled the leotard down over the red marks left by the riding crop, and turned away from Josef. I walked quickly to the door of the communal room, exited through it, and went to my cubicle the way he'd told me to. I shut myself in and lay down on my stomach on my bed.

Then, knowing that no one could hear me because the little room was soundproof, and that no one could see me over the closed-circuit TV because they were all in the communal area, I screamed out my anger. I went into a temper tantrum, pounding the bed with my fists, yelling like a five-year-old, venting my inarticulate rage.

I was still screaming when Josef came and found me five minutes later.

CHAPTER TWENTY-ONE

It took me a moment to notice that Josef was standing there. He moved between me and the light, and I suddenly realized I was in his shadow. I turned around and found him looming over me.

I felt horribly embarrassed that he had seen me venting my frustration like a child. At the same time, I was still furious with him. I lay on my side on the bed, breathing hard and glowering at him. I didn't know what to say.

He pushed the door shut. "I am sorry you found your treatment so disagreeable," he said. "If that, indeed, was what prompted this little display."

I swallowed hard. My throat hurt from shouting. "You're not sorry," I told him. "In fact, you probably got off on it." I felt too angry to try to act subservient.

He shrugged. "As you wish. I brought you your medication, Christina. Everyone else has just been given the daily dose." He held out the white tablet with a paper cup of water.

I realized I had no choice but to take it. I sat up and winced as the raw skin of my bottom rubbed across the blanket on the bed.

"Painful?" Josef asked. His expression was unreadable. For all I knew, he was enjoying seeing my discomfort.

"Of course it's painful. What did you expect?" I reached out for the water and the tablet.

He watched me swallow the medication. "It would have been even more painful if it had been me wielding the riding crop," he said. His voice was very low-pitched, conversational, not at all dictatorial in tone.

I drained the paper cup, crushed it, and threw it angrily across the room. "What do you mean?"

"I mean, Christina, that I protected you from pain as much as I could." He stared at me levelly.

I stared back. "You what?"

He shrugged. "You had to be punished. The Stanowskis would not tolerate anything less."

"The Stanowskis?" I glanced nervously up at the TV camera in the ceiling.

"We can talk for just a few minutes," Josef said. His expression was still totally controlled, but I saw his eyes move warily to the door, then back to my face. "I know that for the next few minutes no one will be watching or listening."

I was dazed by what he was telling me. "Are you really saying that Carl and Helen are in control? That you can't do what you like?"

He hesitated. "There are limits placed upon me," he said carefully. "Christina, do not ask me to reveal more. I ought to tell you nothing. I should not trust anyone. But—" He stopped. Maybe he was just acting again, but it looked as if something was genuinely troubling him.

"I hope this isn't just a line you're giving me to con me, so that I'm the one who ends up trusting you," I said.

He laughed suddenly. "There are so many paradoxes to this situation," he said, looking away for a minute, as if trying to decide how much more to say. "All I can reveal," he continued, "is that I work here within limits. If I were the one who had used the riding crop on you, the Stanowskis would have noticed if I did not strike you as hard as I had struck Mark. They would have suspected me of collusion with you. But I did not want to hurt you too much, so I got Elizabeth to do it, knowing she is not as strong as I am. Therefore, Christina, you shouldn't resent me.''

I studied his face, trying to decide whether to believe him. It did make some kind of sense. "Maybe I resent anyone who makes me call him 'master,' '' I said softly.

He smiled. "But am I not your master? Do you not have to do everything that I tell you to do? When you call me that, you are just admitting the truth of the situation. Right?''

He spoke forcefully again, and I found myself blinking, trying to keep up with him. "I guess—''

"No more talk,'' he interrupted. "Tomorrow, perhaps, we can talk more, if we are careful. Now, Christina, there are other things we have to do.'' Then he stood up, slipped his robe off, and threw it aside.

"What? You expect me to have sex with you now?''

"As usual, Christina,'' he said coldly, "you have very little choice.'' He took my head between his hands, then stooped down and pressed his lips against mine.

A dozen thoughts raced through my head—that I should resist him or even try to hurt him in retaliation for the punishment I had received. But I came back to the truth of the matter: I wanted to know more, and the only way of finding out more was to be what he wanted me to be.

At the same time, though, there was a magnetism between us, which I hated to admit but which was undeniable. Despite my rage at the way he treated me, I wanted him to take me now.

So I hesitated only for a second before I kissed him. I opened my mouth wide and let our tongues touch. I felt his heavy hands clench my shoulders, holding me so tightly I knew I couldn't pull away if I tried. I heard his breathing, smelled his body, and sensed him becoming aroused.

He pulled away suddenly. His cock was already sticking out firm and long. He fondled it while he watched me with his dark eyes, his broad-shouldered, well-muscled body towering above me. "I have to have you, Christina," he murmured. He gestured at my leotard. "Take that off."

He sounded impatient, so I didn't make a production of undressing. I peeled the garment down my body, exposing myself to him while he went on stroking his cock and staring at me with those strangely compelling eyes.

"Now lie down," he told me.

I tried it and winced. "My backside hurts," I said plaintively.

"Then turn over. On hands and knees."

I did as he said. I felt the bed move as he knelt behind me, and sensed the warmth of him as he bent over me and ran his palms down my back, then slid them around to cup my breasts. He squeezed my tits hard, holding them tight up against my body, then squeezed still harder, till I gasped. He possessed me with every gesture, every little action. It would have been hard to resist him under any circumstances. He had such an aura of power.

He kept one hand over my tits and rubbed at my nipples gently but insistently, and with his other hand pushed my knees wider apart. He ran his fingernails up the insides of my thighs and made me shiver with tingles and goosebumps that spread down to my toes. Then he probed the lips of my cunt.

When he found that I was already wet inside, his fingertip began massaging my clitoris even more intently, and I felt the tension draining out of me. I bent my elbows and lay down with my face turned so that my cheek pressed against the bed. I closed my eyes.

"Christina," Josef murmured. "Surrender yourself. Surrender to me, your master."

A couple of days earlier a line like that would have made me laugh, but under the circumstances I was now in, it turned me on. He soon edged a little closer to me and I felt the hairs on his legs against the backs of my thighs.

Then he pushed the head of his cock into me a little way, and took hold of me by the hips. He grunted with pleasure and satisfaction, pushing in a little farther, then farther still, till finally he was totally embedded in me. Once again he reached for my breasts and squeezed them. Then I felt his hand stroking my hair and touching my face.

Soon he was fucking me hard. He plunged into my body with long, strong strokes, then wet his finger and reached around and touched my clitoris. I bit my lip and clenched my fists as my climax began to build inside me. I couldn't conceal it from him, and I think that's why he wanted to turn me on—just for the satisfaction of seeing me unable to fight the heady sensations he was creating within me.

For a little while the only sounds in the room were our heavy breathing, a slight creaking of the bed, and faint wet noises of his cock moving in and out of me. Then, as the excitement grew, I couldn't help letting out a little moan.

Josef paused and pulled his cock almost all the way out. His finger on my clitoris drew back until it barely touched me, tantalizingly, as lightly as a feather.

"Do you want it, Christina?" he asked me in his deep resonant voice. "You want to come?"

At first I didn't answer. But his touch was knowledgeable and insistent. He teased me with his cock, edging it in slightly and making me yearn to be filled by him again. Then, he withdrew once more.

"Tell me you want it," he persisted, "and then, perhaps, you will be rewarded."

I squirmed and tried to push my hips down to engulf his cock, but he held himself back from me. His finger rubbed me quickly, urgently, and the sexual excitement surged inside me. Suddenly, when I was just on the brink of coming, he stopped touching me again.

"Yes, I want it!" I blurted out. "You know I want it."

"You want this, Christina?" he said, pushing into me quickly, to the hilt. I flinched and cried out. He pulled back, then thrust in again. I was in a state of euphoria by this time.

He started pounding into me harder than before. Again his finger pressed on my clitoris, so hard that there was a little pain mixed with the pleasure.

And then his other hand caressed the sore, red skin of my ass. He let me feel just the edge of his fingernails running across the welts raised by the riding crop.

I wanted him to stop—but I also needed him desperately. He knew that; he was completely in control of me. I felt myself rèaching an orgasm, and I knew I was going to come because he had decided that I should. He was making me do it.

Suddenly he dug his nails into my ass. At the same time he rammed his cock deep into my vagina and held his finger down on my clitoris.

I finally screamed, all the sensations combining to trigger my release. Then I twisted to and fro on the bed, my body trembling, the pleasure overwhelming me in giant waves.

Gradually, though, the waves subsided, and I realized dimly that he had come too. Although his cock was still inside me, it was shrinking, and I could feel the warm wetness of his jism.

He pulled slowly out of me and I slumped down on my side on the bed. Though I still had my eyes closed, I sensed him getting up off the bed. I heard his quiet footsteps and his breathing as he moved around me and sat down beside my shoulder.

"Christina," he murmured. He took my face in his hands.

I opened my eyes. His expression was as hard to read as always, but his eyes looked less cold and remote than before. He kissed me gently. I yielded to him.

"You are quite remarkable," he said.

My head cleared, and I more or less came back to reality. I looked down at my own body, then at his. "That was—interesting," I said.

He smiled faintly. "Indeed. We will talk tomorrow."

I sensed that he was ready to say more than he had said before, but then he hesitated and put his robe back on, watching me all the time. At that point I believed I had bewitched him a little, just as his own power had seduced me in some strange way.

He belted the robe quickly, touched me fleetingly on the cheek, and then he was gone, closing the door quietly behind him and leaving me to wonder—if Josef was not solely in control, as he had originally pretended to be, then who was?

CHAPTER TWENTY-TWO

After Josef had gone I showered, changed, and went back into the orgy room. I was hoping for something to eat—I'd had nothing since breakfast.

Sure enough, I found my companions sitting around nibbling the inevitable sandwiches. Josef and the Stanowskis had gone, but before they'd left they'd brought Michel out of his cubicle to join the group.

At first I felt relieved to see him there with the others. But then I realized the condition he was in. He was sitting staring into space, with the same dazed expression as Robert French. Whatever drug they'd given Robert they seemed to have given Michel, too.

"Isn't it terrible?" Alexandra said when she saw me standing looking at the man. "After you went off with Josef, the Stanowskis fetched Michel from his cubicle, brought him in in this condition, and gave a little speech about what happens to people who don't co-operate."

"I see," I said. Privately I was figuring that the Stanowskis' pep talk would have been given exactly when Josef told me he could confide in me for a few minutes in my cubicle, and he was sure no one was monitoring us at that time. Josef must have known that Carl and Helen were in here lecturing the group.

"Are you all right, Chris?" Alexandra asked, putting her hand on my shoulder.

183

I forced myself to stop daydreaming and came back to reality. "Sure," I said, and managed a smile.

Alexandra gave me a hug, and then a kiss on the cheek. She didn't seem to be interested in sex with me—she just seemed to need the physical contact. "Did Josef . . . do anything more to you . . . when he took you back to your room?" she asked.

"Not at all." I hesitated, wondering how much to say. "He just wanted sex, that's all."

She laughed. "What did I tell you? He's hooked on you, Christina."

"Sure he is," I responded. "Sure, he thinks I'm so wonderful, he got that bitch"—I jerked my head in the direction of Elizabeth, sitting nearby stuffing herself with food—"to beat me in front of the rest of you."

Alexandra sighed. "Well, I guess he had to make some sort of example out of you for disobeying orders. Oh, Chris, everything seems to be getting worse. Robert and Michel are like zombies, no one knows what's happened to Mark upstairs, you and Elizabeth have been turned against each other, and none of us knows what to do."

"Did you have a chance to flirt with Carl Stanowski again?" I asked.

"Not really. He gave the lecture, I tried to catch his eye, and then before he left with his sister I went up to him and told him he could absolutely count on me to be obedient and do, oh, absolutely anything he demanded of me."

"Sounds like the right kind of approach," I commented.

"Yes, except that it didn't work. He just smiled that weird little smile of his and looked away as if he was embarrassed or something, and then his sister grabbed his arm and they walked out."

"Well, take it easy," I advised her. "You've only just begun."

"But I don't know how much more I can stand of this," she complained. "Chris?" She looked at me imploringly and put her hand on my arm.

"What is it?" I asked, hoping she didn't want what I thought she wanted.

"I—Chris, I'm so tense, and there's only one thing that would help me relax. You know? Will you come with me to my cubicle where we can be alone together?"

I decided the time had come to tell her what I'd wanted to tell her for a long time. "I'm not really bi, you know," I said. "My real interest is men. I only make it with other women once in a while."

"Oh, absolutely!" she said, with wide honest eyes. Me too, Chris. I wouldn't want you to think I was putting the make on you or anything. It's just that when I'm unhappy, and I don't have a boyfriend—"

"All right, all right." I couldn't tell whether her protestations were true or not, but I had developed a fondness for her, and because of our common plight, I realized what she was feeling. "Just let me get something to eat," I told her. "Then I'll go with you."

A little later I left the communal room with Alexandra. Robert and Michel were still sitting around looking dazed. Elizabeth, of course, didn't speak to me—she just glanced my way and smirked once in a while. And Jane wouldn't say more than a couple of words at a stretch. She seemed worried sick over what was happening to Mark, and I realized she'd developed some sort of a crush on the kid.

The mood in the room was so grim I was glad to get out with Alexandra.

As soon as we were in her cubicle and had shut the door, she was all over me. Before I even had a chance to sit down on the bed she was hugging me and kissing my cheeks, my forehead, my neck, my mouth. The kisses were fleeting and light, yet full of passion and need. She needed to make contact with another compatible human being, and I was the only one.

She pulled down the top of her leotard, then the top of mine. She smiled at me impishly and pressed her body close so that her small breasts were squashed up against my larger ones. I felt her nipples, tight and hard, pressing into my skin. I felt the warmth of her body, its tension and strength. I closed my eyes for a moment and ran my hands down her sides, feeling its contours. She was lithe and supple, and her responses were such a contrast to what I had experienced during my interlude with Josef just a short while before. She was spontaneous where he was controlled; she was yielding where he was dominant.

She kissed me long and passionately on the mouth, her tongue flicking excitingly across mine, then pushed her fingers up into my hair and ground her hips against me. Together, still embracing and kissing, we slowly fell down on the bed.

I slumped down under her on my back. She kissed me some more and then moved down and started sucking on my nipples. Her lips closed around first one, then the other, and she treated me to the most delicate massage with the tip of her tongue, tantalizing and ticklish, sending wave after wave of little tingles across my belly and down to my crotch.

I lay there with my eyes closed, soaking up the sensations. I caressed her auburn hair as she sucked and licked just the tip of the nipple of my left breast. Then she opened her mouth much wider and drew not only the nipple but the surrounding flesh into her mouth. She sucked hard and gently let me feel the edge of her teeth, and instinctively I arched my back and locked my hands behind her head, pulling her mouth harder against me. I luxuriated in the treatment she was giving me. With Josef, there were so many uncertainties and problems, and I always felt he had the upper hand. But now, with Alexandra, there was nothing for me to worry about. She needed me, she wanted to please me, and I could close my eyes and enjoy her devotion.

She took her mouth from my breast and trailed kisses across my stomach, then put one hand over each of my breasts and used her fingers to continue stimulating the nipples, rubbing the skin where it was wet from her mouth.

She shifted on the bed and her head went between my legs. I opened my thighs and felt her tongue searching for my clitoris, probing between my labes, her licking so delicate, gentle, yet insistent.

She found the spot and began sucking and nibbling at it as eagerly as a kid with a Popsicle. She took her hands away from my breasts and slipped them behind my bottom, lifted my hips up, and pressed her mouth down harder upon my clitoris. Even though I'd reached orgasm with Josef not more than an hour before, I could feel the need growing inside me again.

"Move around, so I can do you too," I murmured to her.

She was obviously waiting for me to say exactly that. Immediately she shifted so that she lay upon me with her knees on either side of my head, her mouth still pressed to my crotch.

I raised my head and worked my tongue into her cleft, licking the opening of her vagina. Finding that it was already invitingly wet, I pushed my tongue deeper inside her, then shifted a fraction so that her clitoris was right over my mouth. I flicked her clit with my tongue, nudging it to and fro and up and down.

Suddenly I felt the muscles clench in her thighs and

belly. She shivered and made little whimpering noises, which were soon smothered by the way I was still kissing and sucking her for all she was worth.

But I came first; I think Alexandra was deliberately holding herself back. I reached the peak almost before I expected it, felt the waves of quick, sharp pleasure, and then it was over.

As soon as Alexandra realized I had come, she let go of herself completely. She lifted her head from my crotch, and I heard her gasp and cry out. She thrust her hips down upon my face, urging me to lick her harder. Moaning in a high-pitched voice, she then gave a little scream and grabbed at my body, digging her fingers in as she reached her climax. Then she collapsed as all her strength left her, and she fell upon the bed, gasping for breath.

We lay there for a while, our bodies locked together. Then I shifted around so that I could embrace Alexandra and feel the fronts of our bodies touching all the way down. Her belly was warm against mine; her pubic hair tickled me.

"Thanks, Chris," she murmured, her eyes closed, her breath a faint caress on my cheek. "I feel so much better." She hugged me as tightly as she could, then relaxed again.

"Wonder if anyone was watching us on the closed-circuit TV," I said.

"Let 'em," she replied. "Let 'em eat their hearts out, because there's no substitute for real affection. And that's what we just gave each other."

True enough, I thought—although at the same time I had to admit I had felt oddly empty at my moment of climax. Sweet and gentle as Alexandra was, I needed something more.

As soon as I could, and as tactfully as possible, I disengaged myself from her embrace. I sat up on the edge of the bed and ran my fingers through my hair, untangling it a little. Then I pulled my leotard back on.

"I'm going back to my room," I told her. "I guess I need to think for a little while, or something."

She lay on her side on her bed, with her knees drawn up and a little childlike smile on her face. She kept her eyes shut and didn't look up. "See you later, Chris," she murmured.

I left her like that, never imagining the strange circumstances under which we would see each other again.

CHAPTER TWENTY-THREE

Josef locked us in our cubicles a couple of hours later. I asked him if we were being shut in for the night; he nodded grimly without saying a word. Maybe it was my imagination, but he looked even sterner than usual.

I asked if anything was wrong, but he just stared at me for a moment, then turned away and walked out of my cubicle, shut the door, and locked it behind him, leaving me on my own.

I sat down on the bed, feeling weary and defeated by never knowing exactly what was going on. Also, I was sure it was far too early to go to sleep. Without any clocks or any windows, we never really knew what time it was. But my intuition told me we were being locked away early that night.

Nevertheless, the light in my room automatically dimmed just a few minutes later, so I undressed and got into bed, and after a long while gradually slipped into sleep.

I woke suddenly, convinced that something was wrong. The light in the ceiling was still a dim yellow, and everything was quiet. All I could hear was my own breathing and the beating of my heart.

Then I turned my head and saw that the door of my room was being pushed open. I must have been awakened by the faint sound of a key turning in the lock.

I sat up quickly and instinctively pulled the covers up

to my neck. The door swung inward to reveal Carl Stanowski standing there, wearing his white lab coat. And Helen, right behind him, was also dressed in white.

"What do you want?" I asked. My voice sounded strange to me—tense and uncertain.

Neither of them said anything. They came into my cubicle, pushed the door shut behind them, and stood there in the semidarkness, looking at me for a moment.

"What is it? What do you want with me?" I asked them, trying not to panic. They looked so spooky, as if they had come for me in some sinister way.

Helen Stanowski was carrying a little metal dish. She took a hypodermic out of it. "Just relax and do as we tell you, my dear," she said. "Otherwise, I will have to put you to sleep." She gestured ominously toward my arm with the needle.

I suddenly remembered what Alexandra had told me, about being visited in the night by the Stanowskis. Nothing bad had happened to her; she'd done as she was told. I decided to do likewise.

"Lie down, Christina," said Carl.

I lay down flat on my back.

He pulled something out of his pocket—it was a steel tape measure. This was exactly what Alexandra said had happened to her. Which reassured me—but only a little. I lay there passively as Carl took the covers off me and folded them neatly. After coming back to me, he started measuring me and reading out the data while Helen stood guard with the hypodermic.

This went on and on. Carl measured everything from my height to the diameter of each of my toes. The only time he spoke to me was when he told me to turn over onto my stomach.

Then, when I was finally beginning to relax because it seemed these dumb measurements were all he wanted, he put his tape measure away and told me to get up and come with them.

This made me nervous again. It hadn't happened to Alexandra. "Where are we going?" I asked, trying to sound unconcerned and not doing a very good job of it.

"We are going upstairs, Christina, to visit your friend," said Carl. He grinned as if he'd just made a joke.

"You mean Mark?" I asked. "Is he all right? Why can't you tell me what the hell is going on here?"

"Mr. Bernstein is just fine," said Helen. "There will be no more questions. Come." She opened the door.

Naked, I walked with them out into the passageway. The lights here also had been dimmed. I went with the Stanowskis through the shadows to the main door out of the basement, then we proceeded up to the hallway on the floor above, the hallway where Josef had found me not long ago.

Everything was eerily silent. Helen kept hold of my upper arm in a firm, almost painful grip, while Carl led the way to the door of the room where I had peeked in and seen all kinds of laboratory equipment, and Mark being punished by Josef while the Stanowskis photographed the event.

There was a cold feeling inside me as Carl opened the door of this room. Bright light spilled out. I winced and blinked.

They hustled me into a large space, which was much more cluttered with equipment than I realized. One side of the room was full of laboratory glassware, beakers and other similar paraphernalia, plus microscopes, piles of books, and a couple of file cabinets.

"This way, Christina," said Carl. He guided me toward the big leather-covered table where I had seen Mark stretched out before—I was amazed to see that he was still there now. As soon as I saw him I forgot for a moment my own situation. "Mark! Are you all right?" I called to him.

He was lying on his back, naked, with his hands clasped across his chest; he wasn't tied down anymore. He seemed to be relaxing, taking it easy, with a pleasant smile on his face.

He heard my voice and turned his head. "Oh, hi, Chris," he said. His voice sounded slow and dreamy. "How ya doin'?"

He had been drugged, of course, like Robert and Michel. But he seemed in slightly better shape than they were in, perhaps because his life as a rock musician had entailed taking so many drugs that he had built up a sort of resistance to all forms of tranquilizers.

I touched his arm. "You're really OK?"

"Sure," he drawled. "These guys"—he gestured at the Stanowskis—"they gave me a shot of something, made me feel *reeeeeal* good." He laughed. "And then they brought Janey, here, up to see me."

I looked in the direction he had pointed, and saw that Jane was sitting quietly in a chair on the other side of the room. She didn't look very happy, and there was something odd about her posture in the chair. Then I realized that she was tied to it. She stared at me and I stared back for a moment. Neither of us said anything.

I felt a hand on my arm. "Christina?" It was Helen Stanowski's voice.

I turned to see what she wanted.

"Something for you, Christina," she said.

I glimpsed an object in her hand, then suddenly there was a hissing noise and I was choking on a weird smell. I realized she had sprayed some kind of aerosol at my face, just as she had when she'd first talked her way into my house in Beverly Hills.

I gasped and coughed, expecting that any minute I would pass out—but I was wrong. Within seconds I felt a strange glow spreading through my body, and a strange sense of well-being overwhelmed me.

"What did you just give me?" I demanded. "I want to know, damn it! What have you drugged me with?"

Helen Stanowski gave me her weird, crazy smile. "Just a little something to make you feel good, Christina. An antidepressant which Carl has modified in some interesting ways." Then she gestured to Mark. "It won't make you feel quite as good as Mr. Bernstein, and it won't last as long. What's the matter, my dear? Don't you like feeling warm and sexy inside?"

I steadied myself on the edge of the table where Mark was lying, and tried to take slow, even breaths. It was true—I had started feeling good, warm and sexy all over, as my muscles relaxed. "You gave a shot of this to Jane, too?" I asked.

"No," Carl said, standing behind his sister. "No, she is up here as . . . an observer. But, unfortunately, she has become attached to Mr. Bernstein."

I thought for a second. "So you've got her here to watch me make it with her boyfriend, is that it?" I glanced from Helen's face to Carl's.

"My dear," said Helen, taking hold of my arm again, "you do ask too many questions."

"Yeah?" I asked defiantly. I tried to pull free of her, feeling angry and unable to control it. "Well here's another question," I snapped. "Where's Josef?"

This time there was a perceptible pause. "Josef is resting," Carl said, like a bad actor reading lines from a script. "He told us to bring you up here and deal with you ourselves."

That was possible—but I could tell Carl was lying.

"Hey, Christina," I heard Mark's voice from behind me. "Christina, what's the big hassle?"

I turned to look at him. "Mark, you've been drugged, I don't expect you—"

"Hey, so what else is new?" He grinned. "You got to remember, I'm used to feeling fucked up. I get off on it. You ought to take it easy, Chris. I mean—I know I freaked out a bit myself a while back. But it didn't do me no good, right? So just ride it out, Chris. Go with it. Know what I mean?"

I felt some of the anger and tension drain out of me. Drugged as he was, there was sense to what he said. The more we fought Josef and the Stanowskis, the more we suffered for it without achieving anything. So why fight?

Besides, the whiff of the gas they'd given me was working on me, making me feel thoroughly mellow. "All right," I said to the Stanowskis. "You want me to get amorous with Mark?"

"Yes, join Mr. Bernstein on the couch." said Helen. There was an eager look on her face, and I remembered the video room downstairs behind the smashed mirror. No doubt about it—this woman was heavily into voyeurism.

Well, it didn't bother me too much having an audience; I was beginning to get used to it. I turned back to Mark. "You in the mood?" I asked with an ironic smile.

He shrugged. "They got me so doped I'd do most anything."

"All right, make room, then," I said, joining him on the leather-covered table. It felt cool and supple under me.

"Just take it easy, Chris," he said. "Leave this to me all right?"

I looked into his face. "You sure?"

"Sure. I tell you, I'm used to feeling stoned."

Realizing that there was nothing I could do, I lay down on my back and closed my eyes. Straightaway I felt euphoric. Now that I wasn't looking around me and seeing that freaky laboratory, the drug really began to work on me, and I started drifting into an inner world of pleasure.

At the same time, I could feel Mark starting to do nice things to me. He was going down on me, his tongue working busily where Alexandra's had been not long before. And everything he did just added to my drug-induced feelings of euphoria.

Mark stopped licking my clitoris and lay down upon me. He moved clumsily under the influence of the drugs they'd given him, but I could tell he was trying hard to be gentle. I felt his hands on my breasts, and his hips pressed close to mine. His cock had grown large, and it pushed insistently between my thighs. I opened my legs, reached down, took hold of him and guided him into me.

I heard him grunt and groan with pleasure as I brought his cock inside me. He started moving in a slow, relaxed rhythm, his body rubbing gently across mine, his hips making side-to-side and circular motions. His thrusts were as regular and soothing as waves breaking on a seashore.

He kissed me with the same easy style, taking his time. His long hair fell down around my face, and I felt it tickle my cheek. Dimly I realized that I really liked Mark—under different circumstances, I might have had an affair with him. But now I was beginning to feel drained, exhausted.

"I'm not going to come," I whispered to him. "It's too much of an effort." The gas I'd been given had debilitated me.

"All right, then," he said, his movements gradually slowing in tempo, his hips rubbing gently against mine. Quickly his cock pulsed inside me and he came, as easy and relaxed as he had been all along.

I opened my eyes as Mark rolled off me and saw that

the Stanowskis had been recording the entire scene. Helen was working a video camera, and Carl was peering through some weird kind of gadget like the instrument a surveyor uses.

"The dimensions are far from perfect," I heard him mutter, straightening up from where he'd been peering at me. "There will have to be adjustments." Then he happened to glance my way. "Take Christina back to her cubicle," he told his sister in a petulant, irritable tone.

I couldn't begin to figure out what he was talking about. Was he some kind of measurement freak? I had a sudden vision of a guy who could only get off by measuring people while they had sex. I felt like giggling.

Helen marched over to me and pulled me off the table. "Stand up," she commanded.

My legs were shaky, but I managed to stand. I glanced across at Jane. "I'm sorry, Jane," I said, seeing her grim expression. At the same time I thought how dumb she was to make such a fuss. Why couldn't she just enjoy herself, like Mark and me?

"Come, Christina," said Helen, grabbing my arm.

"Too lazy to come," I mumbled, and laughed stupidly.

"Take it easy, Chris," I heard Mark say from behind me. "I'll catch you later."

"Right," I heard myself reply. I turned back to Helen. "Hey, how long does this stuff take to wear off?"

"The effects will be gone within another couple of hours," she told me.

"Tha's too bad," I mumbled, giggling again.

I let her lead me out of the laboratory, back downstairs to my cubicle. Everything moved around me like a dream. My skin glowed and tingled. I was so happy. . . .

"Sleep now," said Helen, pushing me onto my bed. It sounded like an order.

"I sure will," I replied, as she turned and left me alone and locked the door behind her.

I didn't realize, however, that many more things were going to happen to me before the night was over.

CHAPTER TWENTY-FOUR

Once more I woke up suddenly, not knowing what had disturbed me. I looked and saw the door of my room slowly opening.

But this time it was not Carl and Helen Stanowski coming into my cubicle. It was Josef, creeping softly toward me, looming over me like a giant.

I opened my mouth to speak. Quickly, very quickly, he reached out and pressed his fingers to my lips, while his eyes watched me sternly. He took hold of my shoulder and pulled me up into a sitting position. Then he gestured for me to come with him, out into the hallway.

I found that the drug had worn off, and I was thinking more or less normally. But the way Josef was acting, something was wrong. I frowned at him and wished I could ask him what was going on, but again he touched his fingers to my lips. He then lifted me up onto my feet, and I followed him out.

He walked me to the main exit, just as Helen Stanowski had done a couple of hours earlier. Then he led me upstairs to the floor above.

I saw that Josef was walking very carefully so as not to make a sound. I tried to follow his example, but our breathing seemed very loud in the total silence, and the dim lighting made everything look shadowy and threatening.

Josef walked me along the upstairs corridor. The door into Carl's laboratory was closed, and no light showed under it. All the other doors along the hall were closed too—except one near the end of the hallway. It was Josef's room, I realized—where I had found all our personal possessions hidden in the bottom drawer of his bureau.

He guided me to the door. A single lamp was on, standing beside his bed, throwing a dim yellow light across the room. I walked in, and the sheepskins on the floor tickled the soles of my bare feet.

Josef followed me and then shut the door, taking great care not to make a sound. He paused for a moment, listening. Then he seemed to relax a little. "Sit down," he murmured, and gestured toward his bed.

I went to it and sat on the edge. I hugged myself, feeling cold.

Josef pulled something out of a drawer and threw it to me. I saw it was one of his richly embroidered robes, in scarlet this time, rather than black. I draped it around myself. "What's happening?" I whispered. "What's this all about?"

He walked to the bed, sat down, and stretched his legs out. He folded his arms and stared at me for a moment. "It is time for us to trust each other," he said.

I returned his steady stare. "That sounds fine," I agreed. "But how can I trust you? You've handed me so many lines, you've acted so many roles, I don't know what to believe."

He nodded. "I understand that, Christina. You, too, have been a good actress."

There was a long pause. I suddenly had a sinking feeling that he knew everything about me. He knew how I had played at being his submissive servant. He knew I had been faking it.

He reached for me, dragged me to him, and suddenly

kissed me fiercely. "No more games, Christina," he said gruffly, holding my head in his hands. "You tried to please me because you wanted to influence me. Do you think I am too stupid to see that?"

I avoided his eyes. "Well," I said, "you know, there were other times when I didn't know for sure . . . when I found you kind of hard to resist. I mean, otherwise, I wouldn't have been able to—"

"Yes. And I, too, have felt the same magnetism toward you. That is why I brought you up here now." He took hold of my shoulders and gave me a little shake. "I am being as honest now as I know how to be."

I studied his face, looking for some clue to his intentions. "So what is it you wanted to tell me? Or ask me, or whatever."

He chewed on his lower lip for a moment, as if even now he was reluctant to say too much. Then he shrugged. "Christina, I am not in control here. I was—employed to do this. I am merely a figurehead. The Stanowskis make the rules; I enforce them."

I just stared at him, although my suspicions were being confirmed.

He went on. "In fact, I do not believe Carl and Helen are brother and sister. They are lovers; I know that. She does not allow Carl any other women; he is hers alone. Whether that is the reason she paid for this whole adventure—the kidnapping, the renovation of this building—I do not know. I am sure, however, it is her money. I think she is descended from a very rich German family." He sighed. "There is a lot I do not know, because they will not tell me."

I pulled my legs up onto the bed and shifted closer to him. Now that he seemed to be leveling with me, I wanted to show him at least a little affection. "But I don't understand,'' I said. ''If this place wasn't even your idea—''

''It was not.''

''Then how'd you get involved? I mean who are you, for God's sake!''

He held up his hand and paused a moment, listening. ''Be quiet,'' he told me. ''They are sleeping now, but that woman sleeps lightly. She misses nothing. Every room downstairs is wired for sound. She eavesdrops constantly. I think my own room is safe, but if they caught us, I don't know what would happen.''

He looked grim, and also a little nervous. I saw for the first time that Josef, like the rest of us, felt like a prisoner here. Despite his aura of power, his dominant personality, it was true—he was not in control.

''Anyway,'' he said, ''you asked how I got involved, and who I am. I will not tell you very much about that, because one day when we are back in the outside world, you might use the information to find me. And since I have been an accessory to kidnappings—you understand?''

I nodded.

''But I can tell you how I became involved. I noticed a classified advertisement in one of the Los Angeles pornographic newspapers. It referred to dominance, kinky sex. I am sure it is no surprise to you, Christina, that I have dabbled in that kind of thing. Dominant and submissive behavior in sex is something I enjoy and know well.''

I could certainly believe that part, I thought to myself.

''Anyway, through the ad I met Carl and Helen. They were very discreet, very well protected. They told me of their plan to organize a select group of guests— not prisoners, guests—for an orgiastic colony cut off from the outside world. They told me that they needed someone with charisma to act as a leader. That sounded fine; I agreed. But I never realized that kidnapping was going to be involved."

"You didn't? You seemed pretty happy to go along with it."

He smiled humorlessly. "Christina, as soon as I joined the Stanowskis, they took steps to ensure my loyalty. Do you understand?"

I stared at him, not sure of what he meant.

"Christina," he continued softly, "they gave me a dose of the very same drug that you are now addicted to. I am in the same position as you; I cannot disobey for fear of their withholding my daily medication. Now you see why I was so reluctant to take you into my confidence."

We looked at each other. I saw a muscle twitch at the side of his jaw. Behind his stolid expression I could see just how nervous he was and how isolated he must have felt, unable to tell any of us that he was as much a pawn in this game as we were.

I reached out to touch his face. I traced a line down his cheek and around his jaw, my fingers caressing the dense growth of his beard. "I guess I understand now why you kept coming back for more of me," I said. "It wasn't just the sex, was it? You needed some companionship."

He looked away, and I saw that I had actually embarrassed him a little by making him face the truth. "Yes, it's true," he told me. "I wanted very much to have someone to be with. The companionship of Carl and Helen is not, shall we say, ideal."

I had to laugh at that. The idea of having no one but those weirdos to talk to—it was too horrible to contemplate.

"You would not be laughing, Christina," he interrupted me, "if you understood what they now plan for you and the other women here."

My smile faded. "What do you mean?"

He massaged his forehead with his fingertips. "They are mad, of course. The whole plan was insane, and already it has gone wrong. They never expected the men to be so rebellious and uncooperative. Neither did I, for that matter. I am sure that Carl and Helen thought they would spend a leisurely couple of weeks making their stupid home movies while the rest of us fucked each other incessantly in the orgy room, day after day, without a care in the world. That was their vision. But it hasn't worked out that way, especially since Mark smashed the big mirror. Consequently, they are already planning Phase Two."

"So what's going to happen?" I asked. Without quite realizing what I was doing, I found myself clutching nervously at the bedcover.

"Carl Stanowski is a crank. He thinks he should have won the Nobel Prize, and hates the world for having denied him that. He believes he's not only the best biochemist in the world, but a master surgeon, too. He did cosmetic surgery on Helen, many years back— he told me about it. If you look very, very closely you can see the signs. She is no beauty, for sure, but once she must have been quite deformed. Anyway, Carl is obsessed with female perfection. He has taken it into his head to construct the perfect woman."

"That must be what the measurements are for," I said.

"What?"

"He measured my entire body tonight. And Alexandra's, too."

Josef raised his eyebrows. "Indeed." He paused. "I did not know that. In fact, he must have deliberately done it at night to keep it from me."

"He's a screwball," I said. "You mean, he's really seriously thinking of—"

"He has a little operating theater set up here," Josef said. "I am not supposed to know about it, but I was walking down the hall when he came out of a door that I have no keys to, one that is normally kept locked. I caught a glimpse of the operating room, though I pretended I had seen nothing. I knew I had to warn you, Christina, if nothing else. Maybe somehow together we can think of some way to get out of here. God, I want to get out of here."

He sounded suddenly weary. His shoulders slumped a little, and I realized how much strain he had been under, maintaining his image of stern, implacable power, when deep down he wanted to escape as much as any of us did.

"I thought I could go through the whole thing without too much trouble," he went on, half to himself. "I have taken the dominant role often before, and thought in fact it would be exciting and pleasurable, having seven people serving me, four of them desirable women." He stared moodily across the room.

"Why haven't you grabbed Carl and beaten his brains out?" I said. Then, even as I spoke, I knew why. "I guess he's got the drug supply locked in that safe of his, right?"

Josef nodded. "Of course. And, contrary to what I told you all, I do not even know two digits of the combination of the safe, or the combination of the lock on the outside exit door. Carl and Helen keep that information, and Carl would rather die than reveal it. I know if I threatened him, if I tortured him, even, he would still say nothing. He knows how severe the penalties are for kidnapping, especially in a conspiracy like this. He would be jailed for life, separated forever from Helen, but he would rather die than suffer that. Anyway, he knows that I need him too much to risk antagonizing him. He hands out the doses of the drug that keeps me alive.''

I covered my face with my hands and felt total despair. I had believed in Josef's powerful personality and ability to control everything; it had given me something to hope for. I figured if I got under his skin, he would grant me some favors, and one way or another I'd get the upper hand and escape. Now, however, it was another matter. If Carl Stanowski was my real master and keeper, we were indeed doomed.

"Do not despair, Christina," Josef told me. I felt his hand stroking my arm. "Perhaps working together, we can—"

"Yeah, maybe. Well, I guess it's nice to know you're on our side." I tried to marshal my thoughts. "What about that gun you were toting the day we got off the truck? Does Carl have that?"

Josef nodded. "It is in his safe with the drugs, I believe. He is a careful man, Christina."

"Are you sure he has the gun? If you had it," I persisted, "maybe we could shoot the safe open, get the drugs we need, then break out somehow."

"But you do not have the gun," a voice interrupted from the direction of the door.

Josef and I both sat up with a start. Carl Stanowski was standing in the doorway, watching us. And I knew he must have heard everything.

"Nor will you ever have this weapon," he continued in his singsong, pedantic voice. He was holding the gun in both hands. "I control it, and I use it to control you, and that is the way things will continue to be."

CHAPTER TWENTY-FIVE

"You should have been more careful, Josef," Carl said, walking very slowly into the room. "For two days we noticed you acting differently. So of course we watched you and we listened. We always listen."

I glanced at Josef's face. He seemed completely under control, but I saw the faint pulsing of a vein at the side of his neck, and his heart was beating almost as fast as mine.

"Your empire is falling apart, Carl," Josef said in a powerful voice that betrayed none of his fears, "and you know it."

Carl shrugged. "A good scientist learns from each mistake," he said. "If we fail this time, we will succeed next time. It does not matter."

Josef paused, and I could tell he was trying to figure an angle, any kind of angle, that might work. "So what now?" he asked.

"You will be locked in for a while. We do not know yet what to do with you. Christina will go downstairs to her cubicle. Get up now, Christina. Come with me."

I glanced at Josef. "It was good talking to you while it lasted," I said. For a moment, I felt sorry for him. Although he must have been somewhat crazy to start with—to have answered the Stanowskis' ad and to have been turned on by the cheap power fantasy they offered him—I was impressed by the fact that he had the courage to reveal himself and had chosen to tell it all to me, not to any of the other women. I leaned close and quickly kissed him on the cheek.

"Christina!" snapped Carl. "Come here!"

I stood up. "You wouldn't want to shoot me," I told Carl. "I'd make your place all messy. Lots of blood." I didn't really know what I was saying; the words tumbled out on their own. Being discovered here and being robbed of my very last hopes was too shattering an experience—I couldn't react to it properly. I felt remote, detached from it all.

I turned back to Josef one last time. "Look after yourself, all right?" I told him.

He stared back at me solemnly. He didn't say anything.

I walked over toward Carl. He backed carefully away as I approached. "You will follow me out into the hall," he ordered me.

I did as he said. My mind was still numb with the shock and surprise of being discovered by him.

He ordered me to move down the hall a little, away from Josef's doorway. Then he slammed the door and locked it, keeping the gun in one hand, and watching me carefully.

"I should have thought a guy like Josef could bust out through those boarded-up windows in no time," I said. I guess I wanted to remind Carl Stanowski of how powerful Josef was, compared to his own twisted little body.

"The boards across the windows are one inch thick, Christina. They are held with steel bolts. And even if he got outside, where do you think he would go?"

It was true, of course—out there, Josef would be just as helpless as Robert French had been when he'd tried to run away on the day we arrived.

I leaned against the wall, feeling my defiance subside

into futility. "All right," I said. "What do you want me to do?"

"Turn around. You know how to get back downstairs," he said, gesturing casually with the gun. I noticed he wasn't being as careful with it. He knew I wouldn't try to jump him, but he hadn't been so sure about Josef.

"Sure," I said. "I know the way." Then I hesitated for a moment. "You know, Josef told me some pretty scary stuff. About your—your plans. Is that true?"

"I am an excellent plastic surgeon, if that is what you are referring to," he said, sounding pleased with himself. "I will not answer other questions now," he added. "Walk, Christina."

I shuddered at the thought of him applying his scalpel to me to make me fit his vision of perfection. I turned and walked along the hall. My legs felt shaky, and at one point I bumped into the wall.

"Downstairs," he ordered me.

I did as he said, eventually stumbling back to my cubicle without bothering to look at him again. I slumped down onto my bed, and he slammed the door behind me and locked it.

I wondered vaguely where his sister was, although, of course, Josef claimed Carl and Helen were not in fact related. No doubt Helen had been monitoring everything over their sound and video system.

"You people are driving me crazy!" I screamed suddenly, clutching my head in my hands. "I'm going to end up as insane as you are!"

Then I collapsed and started crying. I felt exhausted, and very, very sorry for myself.

After an hour of miserable sobbing I finally got so tired that I fell asleep.

I woke up when the lights went bright. I'd been dreaming of Gary again, and for a moment I couldn't figure out where I was. Then the knowledge of my situation came crashing in on me.

I lay staring blankly at the ceiling for what felt like a long while, and finally realized there was nothing I could do to help myself; I was as trapped as it was possible to be. Well, I thought, maybe when it came to the final confrontation, I would be desperate enough to make my move wildly and without thinking. After all, at this point I had nothing left to lose.

Grimly, then, I got up, showered, dressed, and waited for them to open the doors. In some strange sense I no longer cared what happened to me, my fellow prisoners, or anyone. I felt like shouting, "Come on! Do your worst!"—because in a sense it seemed they already had.

By the time I heard the key in the lock I was hungry and impatient. It was Carl who came for me. He was moving cautiously, but he wasn't carrying the gun. I thought I knew why: Guns point two ways. It would be too easy for someone to snatch it out of his hand. It was no accident that this place had been designed to prevent us from using anything that could be utilized as any kind of weapon.

"You will join us in the communal room, Christina," he said.

I made no reply and walked past him and down the corridor. Privately, I was surprised that he was going to let me mix with the others. After all, I knew all about Josef now, and I had been told about Carl's plans for the women. I thought he wouldn't want me spreading that kind of talk.

But he caught up with me just before I went into the room. "Christina," he said, catching my arm, "do not share what you know. Otherwise we will make it painful for you."

I turned and looked at him. I couldn't help smiling.

What did he think he could do that would be any worse than what I was already faced with? But I still didn't say anything to him. There seemed no point. I merely nodded to show I'd heard him, and went on into the main room.

I found everyone else already assembled there, with Helen Stanowski and her video equipment moved out of the concealed room and into one corner of the communal space.

Carl entered after me and shut the door. "A surprise this morning, my friends," he said. His voice sounded thin and reedy, and it was weird hearing him addressing us instead of Josef. He looked nervous, too. I could see his eyes moving uneasily behind his glasses.

Meanwhile I was checking who was there. It seemed everyone was: Alexandra, Elizabeth, Jane, and the three men, all of them still looking like zombies.

"Today will be a day of nonstop pleasure," Carl Stanowski went on. It sounded like a rehearsed speech. "We will record it all, as you see. I hope none of you are camera-shy."

He grinned, and I realized he thought he was making a joke. Jesus, I thought, this guy really is crazy.

"I'm hungry," said a loud female voice. I looked and saw that Elizabeth was the one who'd decided to speak up. "Can't we have breakfast?"

Carl waved his hands impatiently. "No, no. Breakfast is later."

"Where's Josef?" Alexandra said. "What's going on?"

"Josef," said Carl, "has become ill. We are looking after him. My sister, you know, is a nurse. He will be fine in a few days."

"Bullshit, man," came a slow, sleepy voice. "That's pure bullshit." It was Mark talking. There was a dumb grin on his face, as if this was all some rich entertain-

ment staged for his benefit, and he was enjoying the
show. "Wasn't nothing wrong with Josef yesterday,"
he went on. "Looked just fine to me. You're bullshitting
us."

The left side of Carl's face twitched in a little spasm.
I guess he could see that controlling us wasn't as easy
as Josef had always made it look. He walked quickly
over to Helen and murmured something in her ear.

Helen nodded. "We will bring Josef down to see you
in just a little while," she said. "That is, he told us to
go on without him. So let us begin now. You will all
undress."

We just stared back at her, all of us, unable to
believe how inept she was at running this thing. No
wonder she and Carl had hired Josef as a figurehead.
Neither of them had the first notion of how to deal with
a group of people.

"Come along!" Carl snapped, clapping his hands.
"You will undress! You did so yesterday, and you did
so before that. You will do so today."

"Well, I'm not doing anything till I get something to
eat," said Elizabeth. She folded her arms with a slow,
determined look about her.

"Me neither," said Jane. She, too, looked grim and
determined. I didn't know what had happened upstairs
to Mark after I had left, but I guessed it had turned Jane
against the Stanowskis. They obviously didn't understand how to impose discipline.

Carl walked slowly over to Jane. I guess he chose her
rather than Elizabeth because Elizabeth looked like the
tougher of the two. "You will obey me, Jane," he
said. "You saw last night what trouble Mark brought
on himself by defying us."

Jane was sitting on the floor with her back against the
wall, her arms by her sides. She pulled her knees up, as
if shrinking away, but there was nothing submissive

about the look on her face. "I saw what happened last night, all right," she shouted. It was the first time I had heard her raise her voice. "You made damned sure of that, you bastard!"

Carl clenched his fists. "Jane, I will have to—"

"Fuck you!" Jane shouted. And then she surprised us all. Bracing herself against the wall, she suddenly kicked him. Her foot slammed up into Carl's stomach, and he reeled backward, waving his arms, and then collapsed facedown on the floor, gasping and groaning.

Jane leaped after him. She had something in her hand—it glinted in the light. Then I saw that it was the shard of glass I'd told her to hide under the edge of the carpet. She'd done it, and never said a word about it.

She fell on Carl, grabbed his head in the crook of her arm, and stuck the point of the piece of glass at the side of his neck. "Don't you do anything," she shouted at Helen Stanowski, who had started forward with a look of shock and panic on her face. "Don't you come near me, or I'll kill him!"

CHAPTER TWENTY-SIX

A small part of me knew that what Jane had done was suicidal, that we should be making peace with the Stanowskis instead of attacking them. But all that meant nothing compared to the pent-up frustration and rage that I also felt.

So when I saw Jane go for Carl, floor him, and stick the jagged piece of glass to his throat, I didn't hesitate for a moment. I leaped up and ran across the room toward Helen Stanowski. My arms were outstretched and my hands were curled like claws.

"Hold her!" Jane shouted. "Hold her, Chris!"

I didn't need to be told. I threw myself at the woman, grabbed her head by the hair and knocked her over by the sheer momentum of my assault. We thumped down together on the floor, and I fell on top of her. Staring into her face, I remembered everything she'd done to me, from kidnapping me onward. It felt so good to see her eyes bulging out at me now with surprise and shock. I banged her head on the floor and jammed my knee in her stomach. I think I was shouting—I can't remember for sure, because there was a lot of noise in the room. Elizabeth was holding her hands to her mouth and screaming; Mark was telling Jane to cool it; Jane was telling Mark to leave her alone; and Carl Stanowski was still coughing and gasping from being kicked in the belly.

Alexandra came running over to me. "Chris—you need any help?"

Helen Stanowski had started trying to push me off her. "Yeah, let's turn her facedown," I said. "Then maybe we can tie her up with something."

Alexandra grabbed one of Helen's wrists, I grabbed the other, and between us we managed to flip her over. "Hold her there," I told Alexandra, "just for a minute. Keep her wrists pinned behind her back like that so there's nothing she can do."

Helen started wriggling and kicking her feet, but it was a futile gesture. "I don't think this is wise, Chris," said Alexandra, and I saw the fear in her eyes. But she didn't know what I knew about the Stanowskis' plans for us. She didn't know how high the stakes were now.

I stood up and quickly peeled off my leotard. Then I used my teeth to rip its hem, and tore the rest of the fabric into strips. "Just tie her wrists together with this," I told Alexandra. "Use it like rope."

I ran over to Jane. Looking at her close up I could see she was scared stiff. But she wasn't about to admit it. She was still holding the mean-looking wedge of glass, which she'd wrapped in a piece of a cushion cover to protect her hand. Carl was lying under her, trembling and cringing from the point of the glass pricking the pale skin of his neck.

"Here," I said to Jane, "you keep holding him there while I bind his wrists together."

"Sure," she agreed.

"Where'd you learn to kick like that?" I asked her as I wound the cloth tightly around Carl's wrists. It was hard to do the job right—my own hands were shaking so much.

"I took self-defense lessons once," Jane told me shyly. "I'm a very nonviolent person. But because of my—my looks, my figure and all, I get harassed a lot. So I learned to protect myself."

"You sure did," I agreed, tying several tight knots in the fabric. The other people in the room were watching me. Mark was still telling Jane and me to "cool it" and "mellow out." Elizabeth was making a pitiful kind of whimpering noise. Michel and Robert were so spaced out they didn't seem to understand what was happening.

"Have you fixed Helen over there?" I called to Alexandra.

"Yes." She sounded very unsure of herself. "But Chris, this isn't going to do any good," she complained.

"That is very true," Helen Stanowski said, her voice muffled by the pillow her face was pressed against. "You are acting like fools. You seem to forget that without our goodwill you all die."

"There's some things that are worse than dying," I snapped back, "such as the plans you and your so-called brother have for us." I quickly outlined Carl's plastic surgery ambitions, for the benefit of everyone else in the room.

"I knew it," said Jane, "I knew it was going to be something like that. When I saw how they treated Mark—"

"I don't believe a word of what you're saying," Elizabeth interrupted, glaring at me. "It's too crazy. I can't believe something as crazy as that."

"Yeah?" I said. "Then let's go upstairs right now and check it out."

Elizabeth stared back as if there was a foul taste in her mouth. "No. I say we should untie Carl and Helen. I think this is all a big, dangerous mistake."

"Jesus Christ," I said. "One minute you want to defy them, the next you can't wait to ingratiate yourself."

"I didn't want to defy them," Elizabeth contradicted me. The whine had come back into her voice. "I just wanted to have some breakfast, that's all. Look, we'll need our medication in just a few more hours. And they've got it locked away."

"She is quite correct," Carl put in. "In fact, we will only give the medication to you if you release us now. Release us and we will forgive you. Otherwise you will suffer. You will die."

"Shut up, you!" Jane shouted. There was something about Carl that really seemed to get to her. She jabbed his neck again with the shard of glass. "You'll tell us how to open the safe where the medication's kept. You'll tell us, or I'll kill you."

"Never!" Carl gasped. "I will never say. And if you kill me, you kill yourself."

I didn't like the way this was going. We'd grabbed the initiative for a few minutes, but we could lose it again if I let everyone get bogged down in a long argument. Logic was on Carl's side.

But I was gambling on my own intuition. Suddenly, I saw how we might have a chance, though I couldn't let Carl or Helen know what had just occurred to me. "Jane, Alexandra—hold them down here for just ten minutes," I said. "Don't let Elizabeth, or any of the men, change your minds. Give me that much time, at least."

"Sure, Chris," said Jane.

I looked at Alexandra. She was the one I was worried about. I could see she was scared stiff and ready to give in. "Alexandra, do it for me," I said, flashing her my warmest smile. "Please, honey? For old times?"

"Well—OK," she agreed, realizing I was her strongest ally.

"Thanks," I told her, then knelt down beside Carl and started going through his pockets. Finally I found his bunch of keys.

"But what are you going to do?" Alexandra called across to me.

"Just follow up a hunch," I said.

"But you're threatening our lives!" Elizabeth screamed at me.

"No—you're threatening mine," I snapped back at her. I started for the door.

"Chris, hey, really, you know, you really ought to try and mellow out for a while," said Mark. He tried clumsily to get up onto his feet and block my way.

I pushed him to one side. "Grow up, Mark," I muttered at him, and strode out of the room.

I knew I had to work fast; the situation wouldn't remain favorable for long. I ran to the door at the end of the basement hallway and started trying one key after another in its lock.

Within a few seconds I hit the right one and pulled the door open. I ran upstairs and along to the door of Josef's room, figuring he'd still be locked in there. "Josef!" I shouted, banging on the panels.

There was a faint response from inside. His bedroom obviously wasn't soundproofed the way our cubicles were. I started trying keys in the lock, but my hands were shaking, and I had trouble keeping track of which keys I'd tried and which I hadn't. Then, finally, I got the door open.

Josef was standing just inside, tensed and poised as if he expected a fight. "Hey, it's me, it's OK!" I told him. "Look—there's no time to talk, but we've got a chance to escape." I was out of breath and so nervous that my throat was almost too tight for me to speak. "Jane jumped Carl downstairs. She and Alexandra have got Carl and Helen tied up. But everyone's scared shitless. They want to knuckle under again."

Josef looked from my face to the keys in my hands, then back again. "I will come and persuade Carl to talk," he said, staring at me with that expressionless, sadistic look I had always feared. There was no mistaking the violent measures he had in mind.

I reached out and pressed my hand against his chest. "You said yourself, torturing Carl probably wouldn't make him reveal anything."

Josef nodded. "I know, but we have to try."

"No, I've got a better idea," I told him. "You've been in his laboratory, right? You've seen some of the drugs he has lying around in there."

"Yes, but none of the medication that we need is ever left out of the safe, if that is what you're thinking."

"No! Look, come with me. Quickly." I turned and ran down the hall to the laboratory door. I started trying keys till I found one that opened it. "Come on, Josef!"

He followed me into the room. "Christina—"

"Just tell me if there's any of that stuff here that they used on Mark or Robert or Michel. Like a truth drug. Or just something to reduce inhibitions. Get the idea?"

He looked at me with new interest. "Of course," he said. "Of course!" He went quickly to the bench where all kinds of experimental equipment were strewn around. He picked up some containers, threw them aside, went across the room to where the leather-covered table stood, opened a couple of closets, and then exclaimed with satisfaction. "Here," he said, picking up a couple of spray cans. "I have seen Helen use these."

"Yeah," I said, recognizing the cans only too well. "So have I. Come on! I don't know what's happening downstairs."

We ran down to the basement and through to the communal room. Josef came in after me, and everyone stared at him in surprise and confusion—I hadn't had a chance to tell them that Josef was as much a prisoner as we were.

"I knew we couldn't trust you!" Elizabeth screamed

out. "You went and got him and told him some story, just to get yourself in the clear."

"Shut up," Josef snapped at her, then grabbed her by the shoulders and literally threw her across the room into a big pile of pillows.

"Jane—Alexandra—it's all right," I said. "Josef's here to help us. He wants out as much as we do. The Stanowskis have him hooked on the same drug that we need ourselves."

"What?" Alexandra asked, standing up, looking confused and doubtful. I could see it would take more time than we could afford to convince her.

"Act first, explain later," Josef told me. He went to where Alexandra had just let go of Helen Stanowski, then picked Helen up, pushed her against the wall, and sprayed one of the aerosols in her face before she knew what was happening. She breathed in—then tried not to—but it was too late. I saw her eyes glaze over as Josef let go of her and she slumped slowly down to the floor.

Josef, holding the aerosol, went over to where Jane was still holding Carl. "Move back, Jane. Let me get to his face."

Jane looked at me for reassurance. I nodded to her and she relinquished her prisoner.

Josef turned Carl over. Carl had already figured what was going on, though—I could see him holding his breath.

But Josef had a quick remedy for that. He drove his fist into Carl's solar plexus, and Carl's mouth fell open and he shuddered on the floor like a beached fish gasping for air. For a long time he couldn't breathe—and being unable to inhale merely made him want to. Finally he managed to take a feeble breath, at which point Josef gave him a liberal dose of the aerosol drug.

Carl slumped down on his back, his muscles limp, a weird smile across his face.

"Christina," Josef said. "Come here and—and fondle him a little."

"How's that going to help?" I asked.

Josef strode across to Helen Stanowski, picked her up, and carried her close to Carl. "You will see," he said.

I decided to do what he told me. While everyone else watched, most of them looking confused and apprehensive, I sat down on Carl's legs and carefully opened his fly.

"No!" cried Helen, in a voice that sounded dreamy and vague. "Stop her! She must not touch Carl!"

Now I saw what Josef had in mind. I had simply thought of drugging the Stanowskis so they'd talk more easily. But he'd realized we could use Helen's possessiveness against her, while using the erotic effects of the drug to make Carl unable to resist me.

I slipped my hand in his fly and pulled out his cock. I fondled it gently, making sure that Helen could see what I was doing. Carl made clumsy movements as if he wanted to sit up and stop me; I pressed my hand against his chest and easily pushed him back down.

"No!" Helen cried again. She twisted in Josef's grip. "Stop her, stop the little whore. Carl, my Carl!"

"Christina will only stop when you tell us the combination of the safe and of the main exit door," Josef said quietly, sounding so reasonable, so fair-minded, as if he were making her a very kind offer.

Helen closed her eyes and shuddered.

I caressed Carl's cock. Being in control of him was giving me a pure, triumphant feeling of pleasure. I held his cock in one hand, licked the fingers of my other hand, and rubbed them persistently around and around the head of his penis. I felt it swell in my grasp.

Then I lowered my head, pushed my hair back so that Helen wouldn't miss seeing anything, and stuck out my tongue and let just the tip of it touch Carl's cock.

Helen screamed. She was obviously fanatically possessive.

"The combination," Josef reminded her. "Tell us, and this will stop." He kept saying that over and over, like a hypnotic command. I stole a glance at Helen and saw that she was, in fact, halfway into a trance.

I ran my tongue from the bottom of Carl's shaft all the way up to the top, licking it as if it were a Popsicle. Gasping and moving his hips, Carl again reached down to stop me, but this time Jane grabbed his wrists. She saw how things were progressing, and she realized what she could do to help. While I continued licking every inch of Carl's cock, Jane took off her leotard and knelt on Carl's chest. She bent forward and pressed her big, fat tits into Carl's face.

"No, stop them!" Helen Stanowski screamed, now getting more and more agitated. "I can't stand it!" At the same time, Josef kept murmuring to her that if she revealed the combination, the torment would cease.

In the meantime, Carl's cock was very hard and wet from all my ministrations. I decided to give the guy the best blow-job he had ever known. I closed my lips around the stiff flesh and sucked every inch of him into my mouth, then opened my throat to him, taking him in all the way. I wriggled my tongue, slipped my hands behind his hips, and soon started moving my head up and down on him in a quick, insistent rhythm. At the same time, Jane took his hands and pressed them into her ample breasts. He trembled and grabbed at her; under the combined influence of the drug and our sexual talents, he couldn't resist.

I felt his cock strain in my mouth and I knew he was close to orgasm. So I took my mouth off him for a moment, looked across at Helen, and licked my lips. She was staring at me in dazed horror. "Hey, Helen," I called to her. "I'll bet Carl will never feel quite the same about you again after this. Now that he's discovered how good sex can really be, he'll be thinking of me the next time he has sex with you. He'll remember how it felt when I made him come in my mouth."

"I will stop Christina, if you just tell me the combination," Josef quickly reminded her.

She writhed and tried to pull free from him, but he held her easily. I smiled at her again, opened my mouth very wide, and brought it slowly down over Carl's cock.

"Thirty-two left, forty-four right, ninety-seven left!" Helen shouted out suddenly.

And that was it. Without a moment's pause I let go of Carl's cock, grabbed his bunch of keys where I'd left them on the floor beside me, then jumped up and ran out of the room. I knew I had to make it upstairs before Josef had a chance to come after me.

CHAPTER TWENTY-SEVEN

I raced up to Carl's laboratory, ran in, and slammed the door behind me. There was a big, heavy bolt mounted on the inside of the door. I shut it quickly, paused, then tried to calm myself a little.

Faintly I heard footsteps coming closer. Then Josef's fist hit the door panels. "Christina!" I heard him shout. "Christina, are you in there?"

"Yes," I shouted back. "I'm going to open the safe, and I'm not letting you in." It wasn't that I totally distrusted him; I just still wasn't sure where his real loyalties lay. Once he had his hands on the drug we were all dependent on, would Josef use his sheer physical strength to intimidate the rest of us and leave us locked in while he made his getaway in the truck outside? After all, as he'd said himself, he was an accessory to some serious crimes, no matter what the excuses were. And we were the witnesses.

"Why won't you let me in?" I heard him shouting through the door at me. He thumped on it again. "Christina!"

I ignored the noise and went over to the big safe in one corner of the laboratory. Repeating the combination over and over in my head, I looked at the dial on the front of the safe. It didn't seem that different from the little wall safe that I had in my own house back in Beverly Hills. I spun the dial several complete turns to

227

the right, then turned it left to thirty-two, right to forty-four, and left to ninety-seven.

Josef was still thumping on the door and calling to me. But I knew Carl had designed the door to be strong enough to withstand this kind of treatment.

I heard a click and grabbed the handle of the safe. This was the big moment. When I pulled the handle, the mechanism made a solid *clunk* noise and the door swung open.

I felt an incredible wave of relief. I knelt down and peered inside. There were the pills: bottle upon bottle of them. Thank God, I thought. Thank God, we can get out of here at last.

I grabbed a couple of bottles, then looked on the bottom shelf and found the gun that Josef and I had talked about the previous night, the gun that Carl had threatened me with.

I didn't know too much about guns, but I knew how to check if this one was loaded. It was. Carefully, I emptied out the bullets—I didn't want to risk Josef grabbing the weapon and using it against me. Then I hid the bullets under a pile of Carl's experimental equipment.

I walked to the door and unbolted it, and stepped back quickly; as soon as Josef heard the bolt slide aside, he turned the handle and threw the door open.

He started into the room, then saw me standing there pointing the gun at him. He didn't know it wasn't loaded, but he still stopped in his tracks. "Christina," he said, with a baffled look. "I don't understand—"

"We'll do things my way till we get out of here," I said. "I'm sorry, Josef. I've had enough of being ordered around."

At first he looked resentful, as if he thought I should naturally trust him. Then he considered the situation a moment longer, and he smiled slowly. "I suppose, in your position, I would do the same," he said.

"Damn right you would," I agreed. "Now, I want you to go downstairs, lock each of the Stanowskis in one of the cubicles they had us in, and bring everyone else up here." I hesitated, feeling weird ordering him around. "All right?" I added, as if I needed his permission.

"Yes," he said, giving me a look that said he was just humoring me.

"I'll wait in your bedroom," I told him. "I opened the safe and I have the drug."

"You are more formidablé than I realized, Christina," he said.

"Thank you." I smiled sweetly. He didn't know how shaky I felt inside. And I wasn't going to let him know.

"I'll go and do as you suggest," he said, then turned and left.

When I heard his footsteps descending the stairs to the basement, I walked quickly along the hall to Josef's room. I went in, opened the bottom drawer of his bureau, and pulled out the box I'd found that contained all our possessions. I picked out my jewelry and put it on, and felt how strange it was how little things like that can make such a difference. At last, I felt restored to something like my earlier self.

When Josef came back with the others, I was sitting cross-legged in the middle of his bed, still with the gun in my hand. "Come in," I told them all. "Come in, come in, let's get this over with. Alexandra, did Josef lock the Stanowskis up, like I said?"

She nodded. "Yes. One to each cubicle." She was staring at me. All of them were. I guess they couldn't understand how I'd taken control of things so suddenly, and what my relationship was with Josef.

"Right, here's what I suggest," I told them. "Obviously we all want to get out of here as soon as we can. But we've got to be careful. I want to see the Stanowskis arrested and thrown in jail, but I don't want to risk taking them with us in the truck. So I want to keep them locked in the cubicles here, and that means some of us will have to stay here to stand guard, while the rest of us go to get help. I suggest that Mark, Michel, and Robert stay here and take it easy while they come off the tranquilizers they've been given, even though there may be withdrawal symptoms. Jane, I assume that you'll want to stay with Mark. And I want Elizabeth to keep you company, because, frankly, my dear''—I gave her a nasty smile—"I can't stand the idea of taking you with me when I leave this place."

"What right do you have," she started shouting at me, "to tell me—"

"Josef," I called to him, enjoying my new commanding role. "Keep her quiet, will you?"

It took him a moment to grasp the fact that I was still ordering him around. Then, smiling as if he enjoyed my act as a new game, he moved to Elizabeth and clamped his hand firmly over her mouth. She struggled, but he held her easily.

"That's better," I said. "So Alexandra will leave with me. We'll have to take Josef, too, because he's the only one who has any idea where we are and how to get back to civilization."

"You trust him?" Alexandra asked. She still seemed shaken and fearful.

"Not entirely," I said. "That's why I'm holding this gun. However, you've got to remember, he was almost as much a victim of the Stanowskis as we were. He told me that he didn't know there would be kidnapping, and when he found out, he couldn't back out because they had him hooked on the same drug that we're all addicted to."

"You've only got his word for that," Jane objected. Josef remained still.

"No, I've watched him face-to-face with Carl Stanowski last night and today. Josef leveled with me and he helped us all. And you've got to remember: The pills I got out of Carl's safe won't last forever. We all have to find an antidote to this damn drug somehow. Come to think of it, maybe Carl knows an antidote, in which case Josef will have to play ball with us and the police to get his own share of the cure. I suggest we make a deal with Josef right now: We'll tell the cops he was just another kidnap victim of the Stanowskis, in return for his help downstairs in getting Carl and Helen to cooperate. Helen might never have talked if Josef hadn't set things up the way he did. And Carl would never ever have talked, in which case we'd be at their mercy now."

I paused to let all of that sink in. I surveyed the group. "Any objections?" I asked.

"I don't know," said Alexandra. "It sounds right, and yet—"

"There is one problem," Josef interrupted. "I don't know the route out of here. They blindfolded me when they brought me here."

I paused. "You have no idea at all?"

"We're somewhere near Death Valley, that's all I know. I did try to keep some sense of the turns we took—I could feel the sun on the side of my face, so I know which way is west. We arrived in the late afternoon."

"All right," I said, "we still have a better chance with you than on our own. Now, in this box are all our jewelry and personal belongings." I handed them around. "Josef, are our clothes hidden away somewhere?"

"Yes, in that closet there."

"You'll get them out for us, won't you?" Again, I gave him the sweet-smile treatment.

With grudging respect for my style, he did as I asked.

Just half an hour later, Alexandra, Josef, and I were all dressed and ready to go. Jane was happy to stay and take care of the three doped-up men and the Stanowskis. And she didn't mind Elizabeth's company. As for Elizabeth, there was nothing she could do about the situation. I was the one with the gun.

I kept careful hold of it while Josef worked the combination lock on the outside exit door. He opened it as easily as I had opened Carl's safe. It swung outward with a faint squeak from its massive hinges.

"It's dark outside," Josef exclaimed. "It's the middle of the night!"

I absorbed this news without too much surprise. All of us had lost track of the time, with the Stanowskis artificially controlling our days and nights. "Do they have any flashlights in the building?" I asked.

"I think so. I'll go look."

Josef came back in a moment with a couple of heavy-duty flashlights. I followed him outside into the darkness. He was being very agreeable, and I thought I could trust him, but I still didn't want to take any chances. I kept my distance, and hefted the gun as if I knew how to use it.

"Maybe we should wait till tomorrow, Chris," said Alexandra. "We could get lost in the dark."

I breathed deeply. It was a warm desert night, and the stars were incredibly bright. It felt exquisite to be outside and free again. "I don't think I could bear to stay in the building," I said. "There can't be that many roads to choose from; let's give it a try. We have to hit a gas station or something before we get far."

"If you say so," Alexandra agreed.

So we said our farewells to Jane and the others, promised them we'd be back with help as soon as possible, and went out into the night. The truck was parked behind the building; I told Josef to drive while Alexandra and I sat beside him in the front seat. I figured that if I was driving, I couldn't keep proper watch over him. This way would be easier.

We got in and slammed the doors. I'd brought Carl's keys with me, leaving Helen's set for the people in the building to use. One of the keys was an obvious match for the truck's ignition. Josef started the motor and turned on the headlights.

"Chris, I can hardly believe it," Alexandra said, sitting beside me. "We're actually getting out of here. I thought it was never going to happen."

"I had my own doubts," I told her.

Josef backed the truck carefully around the building and onto the dirt road that led to it. "Drive slowly," I told him. "This truck's all we've got to save ourselves. I wouldn't want to get stuck or stranded."

We bumped a short way down a dirt road, then followed it around a couple of outcroppings of rock, which I realized served ideally to hide the commune building from view. Then the road we were on ended abruptly where another road cut across it.

"Which way?" I asked Josef.

He frowned and looked first to the left, then to the right. "I think we came here down a hill," he said. "And the track to the left seems to go up a hill. So we should try that."

I shrugged. "Whatever you think."

We made a left turn. It was a difficult path to follow; it wound around and back on itself, deteriorated into a dry riverbed at a couple of points, and went perilously close to the edge of a steep drop. Several times we had to choose between more left and right turns, because the terrain seemed crisscrossed with other dirt roads, all of them looking alike in the shifting shadows cast by the headlight beams.

We climbed a steep incline that forced the truck's motor to labor in low gear. And then, right at the top of the hill, the dirt road that we had chosen petered out. Ahead of us was nothing but sand and scrub grass and cacti.

Josef stopped the truck. "We came the wrong way," he said. "And we are low on gas."

"Damn!" I swore. I was impatient to get this over with, but obviously we couldn't go around in circles all night. "We'd better stop here till dawn," I said. "From here we'll have a better view in the daytime. We don't want to risk running out of gas in the middle of the desert. We've only got enough water to last a couple of days; if we get stranded and no one finds us—"

"True," said Josef. He set the brake and turned off the motor.

"Chris," said Alexandra, her hand on my arm. "You don't think Josef got us lost deliberately?"

"Josef wants to find help just as much as we do," I reminded her patiently. I suddenly realized what I should do. "Here," I said, "take the gun." I put it in her hands. "That'll make you feel more secure. You can stay here in front, with the keys, and keep the doors locked. Josef and I will get in the back." I said this while looking only at her, but I sensed Josef staring at me and wondering what I was up to now.

"After all," I went on, "there isn't enough room in front here for the three of us to rest comfortably. And the back of this truck is full of cushions. Remember?"

Alexandra looked at me strangely. She frowned. "Chris, are you hung up on him somehow?"

I turned to Josef. "What do you think?" I asked him. "Am I?"

"Unfortunately, I think not. Not as much as I once believed," he said.

"But since this is probably the last chance we'll have for any time together," I continued, "and since there are a couple of things I kind of want to work out . . ." I looked at Alexandra. "You understand?"

She shook her head. "No, Chris. But you've given me this." She hefted the gun, which of course she assumed was loaded, like everyone else. "So if you want to get in the back, go ahead." She seemed crushed, and then I realized—she was jealous.

I kissed her on the cheek. "I'll see you in the morning," I said. Then I turned to Josef, the man who had once intimidated me and punished me and made me call him 'master.' "Let's go," I told him, very conscious of the fact that it was I who was in control now, calling the shots.

CHAPTER TWENTY-EIGHT

I got out of the truck with Josef. The night felt magical. A dry, warm wind wafted across the desert and rustled through the scrub grass. There was a moon low in the sky, but the land was almost totally dark—there was no sign anywhere of human habitation. "The Stanowskis sure picked an out-of-the-way location," I said.

"Like Manson," said Josef. "He retreated somewhere near here. With the Family."

"Let's not think about that." It reminded me too much of the craziness from which I had only just escaped. "Let's get in the back."

We opened the door to the rear of the truck. Recalling there was no inside latch, I left the door open after we got in. The pillows were scattered around and everything was just as I remembered. I stretched out and made myself comfortable, and Josef sat down beside me.

"Do you have resentments, Christina?" he asked.

"What, of you? The way you ordered us all around?" I shrugged. "A little."

"I owe you a lot, if you can persuade your friends to do as you suggest and pretend I was just a kidnap victim like the rest of you."

"Yeah, well, I owe you something for helping us get the hell out of there. I'm not making any guarantees, but we'll do what we can, all right?"

"All right." He paused. "Why did you want to be with me here now?"

"Because Alexandra was getting on my nerves. And frankly, because I want this." I reached down and blatantly touched him between his legs. He was wearing tight-fitting pants, and I could feel the shape of his cock. I massaged it for a moment, and then I undid his fly.

"I don't know how you ever managed to act the submissive role," Josef said, smiling.

"Because of the circumstances," I told him. "I had to, so I did. I lived it. On the other hand, where role-playing is concerned, I'm switchable. How about you?"

I kept my tone of voice light and playful, but I knew, really, why I wanted him alone. I wanted to prove that he didn't control me in any way now. That's what I needed to feel: really free.

Josef didn't answer my question. He lay there passively as I pulled out his cock and started playing with it. In the faint moonlight that filtered into the back of the truck I could see him watching me.

His cock was large but limp. I knew that if I was going to resolve this situation the way I wanted to, I had to get him hard right away. I shifted quickly, held his cock up between my two hands, and kissed the end of it. I pouted my lips and relaxed them so that their pressure was soft and sensual. I pressed them down and flicked the end of my tongue lightly over the top of his cock, sucked on him, then opened my lips a little wider and took the head of his penis into my mouth.

He let out a sigh and relaxed a little as I really started work on him. I took his cock deeper an inch at a time, pausing every now and then to tongue it and massage it with my lips. Finally I drew it in all the way, holding its length within my mouth and throat.

When it had grown as big as it was going to get, I pulled my mouth off and kept it hard by rubbing it lightly just with the tip of my middle finger. "My turn now?" I asked softly. With my other hand I toyed tantalizingly with his balls.

"What do you mean?"

"My turn for oral sex," I told him. "Seems like I've given you about twenty blow-jobs in the past few days, so how about if you go down on me for a change?"

There was a long pause. "What if I prefer not to?" His voice was very low-pitched. I knew he wasn't sure of himself in this new situation. Somehow I had the initiative now, and he didn't know how to regain control. Fine; I liked it that way.

"I guess if you'd prefer not to," I answered him, "I'll find it hard to get in the mood for lovemaking, which seems kind of a pity, because it will probably be our last chance." I circled the head of his cock with my finger and thumb, squeezed gently, then moved my grip slowly down the length of the stiff, pulsing shaft.

"Do not try to blackmail me," he said.

"All right." I let go of his cock, swung one leg over him, squatted on his chest, and pushed my fingers up into his thick black hair so that I held his head between my hands. "I'll just ask you straight out. Will you go down on me, Josef?" And I shifted my hips, lifted them up, and eased my pussy toward his face. I pulled his head up to meet me. In the deep shadows I saw his face disappear between my thighs.

For a moment he did absolutely nothing. Then, tentatively, his tongue began working on me and I felt a surge of elation. At last he was doing something purely for my pleasure, for I was sure that going down on women wasn't an act that turned him on particularly.

"Yes, Josef," I said, wriggling my hips as his tongue probed me. "Suck on my clitoris, can you do that? A little harder. And can you nibble me ever so gently with your teeth? Gently—oh, yes.'' I reached behind me and continued stroking the length of his cock. He had started to lose his hardness, but my touch soon restored that. I squatted over him for long minutes while he licked and sucked at my clitoris, and I went on stroking his cock all the while, savoring the moment.

Finally I started getting close to orgasm, and I didn't want to finish the scene just yet. I lifted myself away from his face. His mouth was wet with my juices and his own saliva. He was breathing heavily, a strange look in his eyes.

He started to sit up. I knew he was eager to fuck me; otherwise he wouldn't have done what he just did. But I held him back with my hands pressed against his chest. ''This one's on you,'' I told him playfully. And before he could argue I took his cock and guided it between my legs and sat down on it.

He groaned and reached for me. I guided his hands to my tits—and then seemed to have second thoughts, when he was a mere inch away from touching me. ''You've always been kind of rough,'' I said. ''I don't want you grabbing me roughly tonight.''

He clenched his jaw. I could see how he hated having to admit that I had him in a subservient role. He wanted me too much—that was the power I had over him.

''I will touch you gently, Christina,'' he said in a carefully controlled voice.

''You're sure?'' I let his hands just brush across the soft, yielding flesh of my breasts.

''Yes. Let me touch you.''

I hesitated for a moment more, and then relented and pressed his hands against me. His fingers curled around the full, wide curves of my breasts. But he lived up to his promise; he was very gentle.

I let my full weight press down on him and held his

cock as deep inside me as it would go. I wiggled a little from side to side, scraping my fingernails down his chest, drawing lines through the dense mat of hair that grew there. Once more I enjoyed being in control of the scene.

Then I started moving up and down on him. I tantalized him shamelessly, working him up with a series of quick movements, then pausing, then starting again. I think he knew what I was doing, but he knew how much he wanted to come in me, and he knew I wasn't going to let him have his way. Oh, he could have used his strength to push me off, hold me down, and take me; but that would have been no victory at all for him. It would have forced him to admit, in effect, that I had more self-control than he did, and the only way he could win was by sheer brute force.

So I went on and on tantalizing him, and he lay there proving to me that he could take it. I flexed all the little muscles inside my vagina and massaged his cock with them. I watched the effects that had on him, as he made groaning noises and rubbed the palms of his hands restlessly across my nipples. I clenched my cunt hard on his cock and held him longer, feeling it swell inside me. Then I moved in another little frenzy of up-and-down thrusts, taking him very, very close to orgasm—but not quite there.

Finally I couldn't ignore my own needs. I took one of his hands and guided it down so that his forefinger lay under my clitoris each time I lowered my hips onto him. "Just keep it there," I whispered. Then I started moving my hips in a slow grind, calculated to arouse myself much more than it would arouse him.

It didn't take long for me to reach my climax. My body undulated while each jerk of my hips brought my clitoris lightly across his fingertip. Within a minute I was on the brink; then, exquisitely, I came. I tensed and gasped and shivered and let the feelings take me, while Josef lay under me watching it all.

I sat still for a moment as the spasms ended and I recovered my self-possession. Then, methodically, I started rocking up and down on him. "You now," I told him, and began lifting my hips higher, so that his cock almost came out of me. Then I brought them down hard and fast, clenching my muscles tight around him. I braced myself with my hands on his chest and increased the tempo until he was taking great gulps of air and all his muscles were tensing ready for his release.

"You want it?" I asked. I pulled myself almost off him—and hesitated in that position—poised to bring my hips thrusting down again. "You really want it?"

He didn't answer. He lay with his eyes closed and his muscles rigid. I saw a film of sweat upon his forehead and chest.

I suddenly pulled myself all the way off him. I grabbed his cock and rubbed the head of it back and forth between my labes. "Josef! Do you want it?"

"Yes," he groaned through clenched teeth.

He had admitted it: his need, his desire for me. With savage delight I pushed his cock back into me and sat on him hard. I started fucking myself on him for all I was worth. My hips moved in a frenzy. Our flesh slapped together. I clenched my hands in his chest hair, moving so violently that I saw his whole body shake and quiver.

Suddenly he let out an animal cry, and then another, like a jungle beast. His cock jerked again and again inside me, releasing the pent-up jism. His coming lasted a long, long time, and I loved every minute of it.

When he had finally given me every drop, I pulled myself off him and lay down beside him. "Thank you, Josef," I said, still keeping my voice sweet and light and playful.

He stared into my face for a moment. Then he grunted, turned away from me, and sat up. He put his hands on his knees and stared out of the open rear doors into the desert night.

I lay quietly, enjoying the afterglow from my orgasm and still getting off on my newly regained independence. I watched him through half-closed eyes. His body was a heavy black shape, immobile. He sat there for a long time, his back turned to me as he stared out the door.

I wished for a moment that we could embrace; I would have liked the physical affection. On the other hand, I was pleased by his inability to face me. He knew I had found his weakness and exploited it, and there was nothing he could do. So he sat and watched the night and thought his private thoughts, while I drifted quietly into sleep.

I woke at dawn and felt alert and ready for anything, which seemed a lot different from when I had struggled awake in my commune cubicle and had lain there feeling trapped and helpless.

I saw Josef had fallen asleep at the opposite side of the truck's interior. I looked at his bearded face for a moment, and realized I didn't feel any particular emotions. I had exorcized them all last night. Now I was truly free.

I pulled on my clothes, moving quietly, and got out of the truck without disturbing him. The day was already getting bright and hot. The sooner we got moving, the better.

Now that it was light, I could see that the truck was parked right at the crest of one of the highest ridges around. The desert landscape stretched far away, totally barren and desolate, a mass of jagged peaks and infinitely wide sandy valleys already shimmering in the heat. In the distance, a highway stretched across the valley in a mathematically straight line. I had no idea how to reach that highway. Obviously we had to start by going back the way we'd come.

I looked over the edge of the ridge and realized we'd parked dangerously close to a sheer drop. I looked down and, feeling a touch of vertigo, backed away quickly and went to knock on the driver's window of the truck.

I saw Alexandra's face appear behind the glass. She was bleary-eyed, and her hair was all tangled. I gestured to her to let me in.

The next few moments will always be etched in my memory. I saw her blunder around, half asleep, as she searched for the door handle. There was a muffled thump as she banged into something inside the cab of the truck. I opened my mouth to tell her to get it together, but the words never came out. As I watched, the truck started edging very slowly backward down the incline.

I grabbed at the door handle. "Hit the emergency brake!" I shouted. "Goddamn it, the truck's moving!"

She didn't seem to hear me. She had locked the door from the inside, so I couldn't open it. I tugged futilely at the door handle and looked to see where the truck was headed. It was rolling very slowly toward the sheer drop.

"Open the door!" I screamed. This time Alexandra somehow found the handle and unlocked the door and threw it open. But she didn't even realize the truck was rolling.

"The brake!" I shouted at her. "Hit the brake!"

"What?" She frowned at me as if I were crazy.

The truck was gaining momentum. I grabbed her by the wrist and hauled her out of the cab. She fell down onto the ground and looked hurt and confused, but then she finally saw what was going on. "Get Josef out of the back!" I shouted at her. Then I peered into the cab. "Where's the parking brake?" I'd never driven anything bigger than a station wagon. I was beginning to panic. I was afraid to get in the cab now, because if I couldn't find the brake I'd go over the edge with the entire truck.

I glanced back and saw Alexandra run toward the rear of the vehicle, but she was still half asleep and she tripped. She put out her hands to stop herself from falling, but she hit the open rear door. It swung around and I heard it slam.

At that point, there were just a few feet of ground left between the rear wheels and the precipice. Hanging on, I took a last despairing look in the cab and saw what looked like a hand brake set in the middle between the seats. If I leaped in, I could maybe reach it. But too late, it was all too late.

I had barely enough time to fling myself clear before the truck gathered speed and rolled away past me and Alexandra right over the edge of the steep drop. It scraped its belly as the back wheels went over, and for a moment I thought it might lodge there. But then it tilted and turned and slid out of sight.

There was an awful pause in which Alexandra and I stared at each other, horrified. And then there was a distant crash.

I ran to the edge and looked down. A couple of hundred feet below, the truck had hit the rocks and burst into flames—with Josef trapped in the back.

The next part is hazy in my memory. I remember giving Alexandra some of my clothes to wear, since she had shed most of hers when she settled down for the night. I remember arguing, pleading, begging with her not to try to walk anywhere during the heat of the desert day.

We had no water, she had no shoes. I knew how long we'd last: until late afternoon, if we were lucky.

We found some shade under an overhanging rock near the dirt road that petered out where we'd parked the truck. We sweated out the day, as the heat climbed probably up past one hundred degrees. I thought a lot about Josef trapped in the burning truck, and blamed myself in a dozen different ways. The column of smoke from the wreck continued drifting upward in the still air for almost the whole afternoon.

I worried about the people back in the commune building, and how we would ever be able to save them now. I figured maybe we could walk there when it got dark and the heat eased off. I thought of Gary, and cried a little, and then made myself stop because I was getting so dehydrated in the heat that even shedding tears seemed like a terrible waste of body fluid.

We both became a little crazy because of the heat. In the late afternoon I thought I was hearing things: strange buzzing noises in my head. I drifted into a half sleep, and then—luckily, very luckily—I managed to wake myself up. I opened my eyes just in time to see a Jeep bounce up the rough dirt road, its motor roaring. That was the noise I'd thought was imaginary.

I ran out, screaming and waving. There was a ranger in the Jeep, and he saw me, thank God.

It seems we were right on the edge of a national wilderness area, and the rangers had noticed the smoke from the wrecked truck. They had come to check it out and pick up anyone who'd survived.

The survivors, though, were only myself and Alexandra. Josef was found dead.

CHAPTER TWENTY-NINE

The phone rang. "Damn," I said. "Look, Gary, I have to answer it. I'll be back in a second, I promise."

I got up and strode quickly out of my bedroom, down the hall and to the kitchen. I could have taken the call on my bedroom phone, but I thought I knew who it was, in which case I needed privacy.

It was Robert French, just as I had expected. "Christina!" His lawyer's baritone bellowed down the line and made me hold the receiver away from my ear and wince. I remembered when, just a week or so ago, the guy had been reduced to a mumbling zombie. In a way, I thought, it was too bad that the monster doses of tranquilizers he'd been given had had only a temporary effect. Now that he was back to his everyday self, he was pretty hard to take.

Still, he had good news. "Carl Stanowski finally cracked," he told me. "We got the bastard to admit it, Chris. He does have an antidote for the pills he made us dependent on. Just wanted to tell you right away. We don't have to worry anymore about the supply running out."

As he spoke, I realized that there had been a continuous knot of tension in my belly ever since we'd gotten back to the everyday world and I'd returned to my Beverly Hills home. Now, listening to French, I felt that tension go away.

"That's great news, Robert," I agreed. "The cops finally got the Stanowskis to admit to everything?"

"Yes. Everything. He's a wreck, Chris." French sounded as if he relished the thought. "He's fallen into more or less the same condition that he put me into. Except in his case it may well be permanent." French laughed nastily.

Delightful sense of humor, I thought to myself. Still, I realized French was the type of guy we needed as a lawyer, and he'd won himself the job, just as he always claimed he would. I decided I wouldn't want to be in Carl or Helen Stanowski's position when they ended up facing French across the courtroom.

"So when do we—" I began.

"Grand jury hearing in a couple of days, which is just a formality in this case. The publicity will start then, Christina. No way to avoid it any longer. This case is just too big. Hell, it's the kidnapping drama of the century."

"Yes," I said without too much enthusiasm. I figured maybe I could leave for Monte Carlo; they had enough witnesses without me. "Well, Robert—"

"I know, I know, I talk too much, right? I just wanted to tell you, though. Oh, incidentally, we've finally nailed down Carl Stanowski's background. His real name is Heinrich Mueller. He was a research chemist for a big pharmaceutical company, till they threw him out for unauthorized experiments on human guinea pigs. When he left the company he took a lot of his experimental samples with him."

"And that's what he used on us? Ugh!"

"Right. Anyway, we'll meet tomorrow and take the antidote to the stuff." French then went rambling on about where and when we'd get together, as if it were a high school reunion.

I got him off the line as soon as I could. I wasn't

looking forward to meeting all my one-time fellow prisoners again.

I hung up the phone and went back to my bedroom.

"Business?" asked Gary. He was lying stretched out naked on the white satin bedcover. His clothes and mine were in a tangled pile on the floor where we'd thrown them just before the phone rang.

"Not exactly business," I said. "Legal stuff."

"You're a mysterious person, Christina. You still haven't really told me where you've been hiding for the last ten days. I began to think I was never going to see you again."

"Yeah. I was beginning to think that too," I said with feeling. I sighed. "Gary, I'll tell you the whole story within the next week or so. But right now I want to forget it. I want to live just for the present. It's such a relief seeing you again, and being back here."

I think he could tell I was sincere. He rolled over, got up off the bed, and walked to me. The bright California sun was shining through the big windows behind him and making his hair gleam with a golden halo. He moved lightly on his feet, and I realized how hung up I still was on his looks and his style.

He reached for me and hugged me, then kissed me on the mouth, insistently and thoroughly, and I felt him opening the front of the terry-cloth robe I'd put on to go answer the phone. His hands closed upon my breasts.

For a moment I remembered how Josef had touched me there, during those awful days when I had been his prisoner. But that was a dark memory, linked with his horrible death, and I shut it all away in the back of my mind. I returned to the present, here in my own home with Gary.

He cupped my breasts, squeezed gently, and looked down at the double handful. "I want to go someplace elegant with you tonight, Chris," he said. "I want you to wear a low-cut dress, something outrageous that'll really show off your figure. I want everyone to see who I'm with, and I want them to be jealous."

I kissed him on the cheek. "All right," I agreed. I felt flattered; after all, he was the movie star, not me.

He kissed the tops of my breasts, then held them up and kissed one of the nipples. His lips closed around it and he nibbled lightly at the little bud of flesh, sucking and tonguing and kissing some more. Soon he grasped me more firmly and buried his face in my tits, nipping the flesh teasingly with his teeth, then licking and kissing the sensitive skin and sending wave after wave of tingles across my belly.

I stood there letting him do it to me. I shrugged off the robe, and it fell behind me on the floor. I ran my fingers through Gary's hair and traced the powerful lines of his shoulders. "Let's get into bed," I whispered to him.

Moments later we were twined together on the cool, smooth silk sheets. He was kissing me fiercely, without any inhibitions. I could feel the intensity of his passion. He made no secret of his powerful, hungry need for me.

I was already very aroused. I kissed him back with the same passion he showed for me. I reached for his cock and rubbed it quickly, impatiently, eagerly. I opened my legs, rolled on top of him, and trapped his cock between my thighs. Then, in one quick movement, I put him inside me.

We lay locked together for a moment. I held him down with my weight and wouldn't let him move while I felt his cock stiffen and strain inside me. I rubbed my tits across his chest and kissed him some more, feeling his passion grow to the point where he couldn't contain it.

"Tantalize me, would you?" he said with a grin. He suddenly hugged me tightly to him with both arms, then reared up and rolled me onto my back, still with our bodies locked tight together.

I giggled and wrapped my legs around his hips, still trying to stop him from moving. But he playfully reached behind and tickled the sole of one of my feet.

He had me then. He fucked me hard, and I moved my hips to match every thrust. He took me with eager lust, and gave himself totally to the experience, moving intuitively, his lithe body responding with a heady mixture of power and beauty.

I buried my face in the side of his neck and breathed in the smell of him, which was intoxicating. I closed my eyes and let those strong, sweet sensations take over and guide me. I no longer was aware of the details of what each of us was doing. I surrendered to the mood of the moment.

His thrusts speeded up, and he fucked relentlessly, in a flurry of passion. My arousal became a nagging, irresistible tension that wouldn't go away, and I gasped and cried until I finally came, writhing against him. I guess seeing me reach my climax turned him on too, because he had his own almost simultaneously. Feeling the spasms of his cock inside me, I opened my eyes and saw his face contorted in a moment of pure pleasure. Then he fell down upon me, and for long minutes we rested together.

"Welcome back, Chris," he said finally, and rolled so that we lay side by side. He caressed the curves of my breasts, then reached down and grabbed my ass, pulling me snugly against him. "I missed you," he said.

"There'll be no more sudden departures," I told him. "I promise."

He kissed me tenderly.

At that very moment, my doorbell rang and Gary

broke the kiss. He opened his arms to let me get out of bed and go to the door.

"Forget it," I said, as the bell rang a second time. "I answered the door once before . . . and it was bad news. This time, I know better. I'm staying right here in bed with you." And then, before he could ask any questions, I kissed him again.